"I'm so s⋯⋯⋯⋯⋯⋯rted, but the m⋯⋯⋯⋯⋯⋯n's reach, Ril⋯⋯⋯⋯⋯⋯er.

Their lips crashed together with a smack that echoed. Riley threw her arms around the man's neck like he was a lifeline and she was on the brink.

The kiss was hard, but it unfurled something inside of her that she didn't realize had been there in the first place. Her unexpected weight against him sent them backward to the concrete she realized she'd now despise forever. Her arms around his neck kept his head from connecting with that same floor.

Riley ended the kiss as quickly as she'd initiated it.

Then she was lying on top of the man and staring into his eyes.

"Thank you," she said, breathless.

Thank you for not letting a man die because I couldn't hold on.

Thank you for not questioning me when I needed you to do something.

Thank you for coming back.

IDENTICAL THREAT

TYLER ANNE SNELL

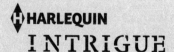

HARLEQUIN
INTRIGUE

This book is for Alaina D. You let me talk about twins before,
during and after this book was written like it was normal…and
never once complained. Thank you for being a supportive
friend during a very frustrating time in my life.
I couldn't have asked for better.

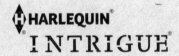

ISBN-13: 978-1-335-13594-0

Recycling programs
for this product may
not exist in your area.

Identical Threat

Copyright © 2020 by Tyler Anne Snell

This edition published by arrangement with Harlequin Books S.A.

For questions and comments about the quality of this book,
please contact us at CustomerService@Harlequin.com.

Harlequin Enterprises ULC
22 Adelaide St. West, 40th Floor
Toronto, Ontario M5H 4E3, Canada
www.Harlequin.com

Printed in U.S.A.

Tyler Anne Snell genuinely loves all genres of the written word. However, she's realized that she loves books filled with sexual tension and mysteries a little more than the rest. Her stories have a good dose of both. Tyler lives in Alabama with her same-named husband and their mini "lions." When she isn't reading or writing, she's playing video games and working on her blog, *Almost There*. To follow her shenanigans, visit tylerannesnell.com.

Books by Tyler Anne Snell

Harlequin Intrigue

Winding Road Redemption

Reining in Trouble
Credible Alibi
Identical Threat

The Protectors of Riker County

Small-Town Face-Off
The Deputy's Witness
Forgotten Pieces
Loving Baby
The Deputy's Baby
The Negotiation

Orion Security

Private Bodyguard
Full Force Fatherhood
Be on the Lookout: Bodyguard
Suspicious Activities

Manhunt

Visit the Author Profile page at Harlequin.com.

CAST OF CHARACTERS

Desmond Nash—As one of the Nash triplets who were abducted when they were eight, this charming cowboy has come back to his hometown to put down roots and expand his business. But after a chance encounter places him between a beautiful woman and a dangerous threat, he finds the line between the past and the present has blurred for everyone. Not just him.

Riley Stone—After a mistake in identity has her in the right place at the wrong time, this twin goes from wanting to blend in to hoping her family can survive whatever danger has followed them into their fresh start. When the mystery seems to be connected to the cowboy with the baby blue eyes, she has to decide to either take on the past or risk their future.

Jenna Stone—As Riley's identical twin, she is often mistaken for her sister. Sometimes even by family.

Declan Nash—Sheriff and the triplets' older brother, this lawman has to figure out if the person causing trouble is a new threat or a ghost from the past.

Hartley Stone—Jenna's toddler son loves his aunt Riley just as much as she loves him.

Caleb and Madi Nash—The brother and sister who complete the Nash triplets. The detective and innkeeper will do anything to keep their family safe.

Man in the Suit—He isn't the first mysterious, well-dressed figure to appear in Overlook, but he certainly seems to be pulling some of the strings this time around.

Chapter One

The unmistakable truth was that the woman who had just entered the party wasn't a local. The very mistakable truth, however, had to do with her intentions for being there in the first place.

Was she a prospective donor for one of the nonprofits they worked alongside?

Was she there to ask how the Second Wind Foundation would operate now that it was moving its official headquarters to the town of Overlook, Tennessee?

Was she a Wildman County reporter?

Was she there as someone's date?

Desmond Nash tried to keep his attention on the small group of guests who had crowded around him like he was some kind of animal on display at the zoo, but it was hard not to keep track of the woman as she split through the party with practiced ease. The descriptor of *siren* lodged itself in Desmond's head at the sight of her.

Long tangles of dark red curls flowed across her shoulders and back, water infused with the very concept of mystery. Her brows matched, thick and sculpted, hooding dark eyes that, even from the distance between her and Desmond, pulled at him. Without the tall heels she wore pushing her height up a few inches, he supposed he would have to tilt his chin down to see into those dark eyes.

The interest certainly didn't stop there. The way she carried herself spoke of confidence and grace. Like the rest of the outdoor gala attendees, she was wrapped in a dress meant only for special occasions. Black silk contrasted against her pale and freckled skin, dipping low at the chest and clinging to the curves of her hips.

Whoever the woman was, she was commanding the outdoor gala just by existing.

"We're just so glad you decided to come home, Desmond."

His name was what finally broke the trance he'd fallen into looking at the newest guest. Desmond turned to the deep voice of Garfield Taylor, one of the town council members and once a very good friend of Desmond's father, Michael.

"You've been going nonstop since you started Second Wind," Garfield continued. "Maybe now since you're back it's time you finally slowed down?"

It was said with a twinkle in his eye and a slight tease in his tone. The older man cut his gaze to where Desmond had just been staring.

He grinned. Desmond had been caught gawking at the new arrival. Now he'd given Garfield the perfect excuse to ask what his mother had already been asking without actually saying the exact words.

When are you going to settle down?

If Desmond had been one of his brothers—their tact was all but absent when it came to someone trying to pry into their personal lives—he would have responded in a saltier manner.

I'll slow down when you show me that book of yours you've been working on for ten years, he wanted to say.

Instead Desmond chose a more diplomatic response.

"Second Wind is just as much a part of my life as this ranch," he said, pulling up an easy smile. "As long as there are people out there I can help, I don't think slowing down is an option for me."

The group around them started smiling; some laughed; most everyone had a drink in hand. Garfield was grinning but didn't press the issue. Instead another Overlook local took the floor and, thankfully, kept it to the topic of work. Desmond was prepared to go over Second Wind's construction schedule for the umpteenth time that night but a slight tug at his elbow gave him an excuse to switch gears. A pair of blue eyes that matched his to a *T* stared up through long lashes at him.

"Sorry to interrupt but can I pull you away for a second, Des?"

Madi knew she could do just that without apologizing. Whereas he was the star of this particular party, Madeline Nash was just as infamous as he was. Being a local was synonymous with knowing every detail about the Nash family.

Specifically, Desmond, Madi and Caleb.

It was a fame none had asked for and yet one they couldn't escape. Even if they moved off the ranch and married into a new last name as Madi had.

"Sure," Desmond said. He tipped his Stetson to the group. "Excuse me, folks."

Madi led him a few feet away before she spoke, waving at him to follow her as she did. Desmond didn't need a triplet connection with Madi to know she was headed toward the sweet tea bar. Most of the guests had champagne flutes. Madi Nash was about to have a mason jar of Milo's.

"I didn't really need anything," she said, eyes on target. "I just felt like you needed a break from that particular crowd. I saw the way Garfield was looking at you. Not to mention Missy. I'm pretty sure she was two seconds from drooling on you."

Desmond chuckled.

"I didn't notice Missy but I do thank you for the save from Garfield. And talking about the construction again. It's been the most-asked question of the night other than *What's next for Desmond Nash?*"

It was Madi's turn to laugh. She slowed as she neared the bar and Desmond couldn't help but take the atmosphere all in again.

The outdoor gala had been set up by an event company out of Kilwin, the city next to Overlook. They'd erected giant and, dare he think it, classy tents across the field between the main house on the ranch and the horse stable. They'd taken a field of grass and dirt and somehow made it into a high-class event. Set against the backdrop of mountains, forests and stars and everyone's tuxes and dresses, it all just seemed to work.

Desmond was definitely impressed, even more so with the catering staff.

They were local and they kept up casual conversation with most of the guests as they bustled in and out of the designated food-prep area. Matthew Jenkins bebopped past them with another tray of drinks. He nodded to Desmond and tipped his hat to Madi. It was an interesting contrast to the image Desmond had of the same man but years younger, drunk as a skunk and trying to tip Mr. Elroy's cow because he saw it in a movie once.

"Overlook isn't used to a good kind of excitement," Madi said, smiling at the attendant in charge of filling the jars with tea. "You, not only coming home, but literally building a three-story structure for Second Wind right here in town is a big deal. If you think you're going to be able to smile away that type of hype, you're foolin' yourself there, cowboy."

Madi wasn't wrong. Overlook was a small town. They got by, sure, but there hadn't been a new business that had set up shop on the same scale as Second Wind. Construction had roughly two months left, and every time he'd been to the site to see the progress, he'd seen at least two or three bystanders checking it out too.

Madi also wasn't wrong about the excitement part either. Overlook had had one heck of a streak of chaos in the last few years. The fact that it had all revolved around the Nash family only threw more fuel on the gossip-and-talk fire.

"I know, I know," he conceded. "But it would be nice if they at least shook up the conversation. Dressing up in a suit makes my skin crawl—dodging personal questions only makes matters worse."

Madi took her sweet tea with a smile. Desmond once again followed her.

"You can't get all hot and bothered about those kinds of questions," she said, keeping her voice low as they navigated around a pocket of guests next to one of the buffet tables. "They're all just wondering why the most charming and sweet-talkingist Nash doesn't have a plus-one dangling on his arm."

Desmond sighed. It earned another laugh. "You better find yourself a better answer than annoyance," Madi continued. "Now that you're living full-time in Overlook, every single one of Ma's friends are going to start parading their unattached daughters up Winding Road and right to your front door. And they won't take any sighs for answers."

Desmond thought of the siren. He almost asked if Madi had seen her too when her path led them right to Julian Mercer.

He was often described by Madi as "a mountain of a man" and the description was apt. Desmond was a tall man and yet he had to tilt his chin up a fraction to stare his brother-in-law in the eyes.

"Extraction successful," Madi said, conspiratorially.

"No casualties?" Julian played along.

"Other than Missy's pride? None."

Julian looped his arm around Madi and pulled her into his side. He was smiling, just as he always was when Madi was near.

An ache of loneliness reminded Desmond that he hadn't had that kind of closeness, or any kind really, in a long time. Second Wind wasn't just his livelihood, it had become his entire life in the last few years. His late nights were spent with facts and figures, his dinner dates with potential investors and his holidays with ideas of what to do next.

Moving back to Overlook hadn't originally been his idea. In fact, it had been the family's.

"You need a connection to something outside Second Wind," his mother had said. "Trees can't grow without roots. You need to attach somewhere. Why not in Overlook?"

Now here he was, trying to keep his eye on the professional ball while letting invisible tree roots dig into the ranch ground.

"You two are a hoot," Desmond deadpanned. It only made the couple smile wider.

"We'll be here all night," Madi teased. "Available for dinners too."

They devolved into playful bickering followed by the appearance of Overlook's sheriff, the eldest Nash sibling.

Declan Nash looked even more uncomfortable wearing a suit than Desmond did. He gave them a gruff greeting. He wasn't one of the triplets but that didn't mean they weren't just as close with him as each other. Madi's brow creased in concern just as Desmond voiced what she was thinking.

"What's wrong?"

Julian, not as well-versed in all of the subtleties of the family yet, tensed. Desmond angled his body so they were in a huddle-like circle.

Declan sighed. It was his trademark move.

"It's nothing but it's something."

Something happened but it wasn't a big deal. Desmond felt his brow raise.

"Be more specific and I can agree with you," Desmond prodded.

Declan sighed again.

"I just got back from the construction site. There's been some vandalism on one of the first-floor exterior walls."

Desmond clenched his jaw. Declan continued. "It's nothing that a little gray paint can't fix but it's also nothing you want showing out to the road. Caleb and I were on the way here when the call came in so we went over and covered it with a tarp. That's why we're late."

"What was it?"

Declan shook his head.

"Just some idiots being idiots. Nothing you need to deal with right now."

"You have security cameras, right?" Julian asked.

"Interior cameras, but the law office across the street has one pointed at the building. Marty McLinnon works there. He's actually here at the party. I can go ask him if we can get the footage?"

Declan took off his cowboy hat and shook his head.

"Let me go see if I can't find him. If not, this can wait until tomorrow. Don't worry."

He clapped Desmond on the shoulder and

headed off to the tent that housed the most people mingling. Before he could penetrate the main group he was called this way and that by his constituents. Desmond might have been dubbed the "most charming" Nash but as sheriff Declan had his own claim to fame.

"He didn't tell me what was put on the wall," Desmond realized.

Madi's gaze went over his shoulder. Her cell phone started to ring as she spoke.

"There's Caleb… And this is the babysitter with an update since I'm a neurotic parent." Madi and Julian moved farther away from the party to take the call as Desmond turned to the last Nash sibling.

Caleb was half Declan, half Desmond. He was a detective at the sheriff's department and smart as a whip. Like Declan, his love of law enforcement was ingrained in him. However, like Desmond, he was more inclined to lean on humor and lightheartedness when managing the rest of his life. That separation had become more pronounced after he'd met his wife, Nina. As he scanned the crowed, Desmond knew she was who he was looking for.

Too bad Desmond was about to bombard him with questions that led straight back to the work side.

The live band in the main tent started up a slow song that leaned into a piece of piano music. It didn't pair well with the tension now lining his shoulders. Desmond didn't care. He had Caleb in his sights, tunnel visioned in.

Second Wind meant more to him than people seemed to realize. It was a lifeline for some. It was a lifeline for him.

After everything his family had been through…

After the abduction.

After his father's death.

After years of therapy, physical and mental.

After realizing the fallout of what had happened might never stop coming.

Second Wind might have been a foundation that helped nonprofits who in turn helped others with precision and expertise, but it was so much more for Desmond.

It might have seemed idiotic that something as small as vandalism that could be covered with a little paint had completely derailed his entire focus, especially at a party, yet it had.

So much so that he nearly ran into a guest who found her way into the path between him and Caleb. She'd been staring up at the tent's ceiling.

"Oh, excuse me," Desmond said, stopping so suddenly he had to put a hand on her arm to keep them from colliding farther. The woman reached a hand out to his chest to keep the same collision from happening, clearly startled.

It was the siren.

Her face flushed. Her dark eyes widened.

"No, excuse me," she said with a nervous

laugh. "I'm the one walking around in here staring at these tents without looking where I'm going!" Recognition flared behind her eyes. Her cheeks turned an even darker shade of crimson. She dropped her hand and took a step away from him like she'd been bitten. "And you're Desmond Nash, the host. Wow. Talk about an embarrassing first impression."

"I'm actually happy someone else is in awe of these," he said, pointing up. "I'm not about to be upset at someone else for doing what I was ten minutes ago."

She still looked nervous but she smiled all the same.

"Well, I might as well introduce myself now." She extended her hand. "I'm Jenna Stone."

The name was familiar.

Yet, Desmond couldn't place it.

A look that seemed to reach way past worried flashed across her expression. She dropped his hand quickly and took another step backward. Desmond almost turned around to see if it was someone else who had caused the almost scared reaction.

"I'll let you get on your way," she hurried. "I think it's time I checked out the band now."

Desmond opened his mouth to say something—he wasn't sure what—but Jenna was fast.

One second she was there.

The next he was standing alone.

Chapter Two

It was a lie.

She was *not* Jenna Stone but, boy oh boy, had she said it.

Out loud.

To another human.

To *him*.

No. She was Riley Stone, Jenna's sister. Her twin to be exact. Identical in every physical aspect—well except for the tattoo she'd gotten her first spring break in college that her parents *still* didn't know about—the Stone sisters were nearly indistinguishable.

Which was why Riley was at the Nash family ranch, attending an extremely fancy gala wearing an extremely tight dress and trying to limit the amount of lies she was telling.

To help her sister she had to *be* her sister. At least for the night.

But then she'd gotten swept up in the atmosphere and literally run into the man who had made the party possible.

Desmond Nash looked nothing like he did on the foundation's website. The professional portrait had shown a commanding man with gelled dark hair, cold blue eyes and a smile that said he knew exactly how much he was worth. His bio, with its lists of every successful business venture he'd run before starting Second Wind, only backed up the image of a businessman who never bit off more than he could chew. In person, however, the intimidating image Riley had held since that morning's briefing by her sister had slightly skewed.

He wore a suit but his cowboy hat threw off the uptight business ensemble, just as his messy hair and carefree laughter had tipped the scale from consummate professional to normal, well-dressed man with a smile that had done something to Riley's stomach when she'd seen it. His eyes had crinkled at the corners and those baby blues had seemed a lot warmer when she had been close enough to touch him.

Desmond Nash was not what she had expected.

All you have to do is be present, Jenna had coached earlier that day. *Go in, eat and drink, mingle, smile and make small talk. That's it.*

Riley wanted to bean her sister on the head. She wasn't a fan of deception, even if it was for a good cause. Lying, well lately it had taken on a new face for Riley. It meant something else. It hurt more. It angered her more. Now she was moving through a party filled with guests who didn't even suspect she was effectively a walking and talking lie.

It's not that big of a deal, Riley tried to assure herself. *Jenna couldn't come so we did a weird version of* The Parent Trap. *It's not like we're trying to grift or anything.*

The inner pep talk didn't completely land but Riley raised her chin and moved on to the next tent, following a beautiful piano medley.

Overlook was much like the Nash family ranch which was *also* much like Desmond. Riley hadn't expected to be surprised and impressed with any one of them.

A small, small town in mostly rural Tennessee, Overlook was a far cry from Riley's last home of Atlanta, Georgia. There was no constant hustle or bustle, no tall buildings of metal and glass, no concrete jungle, no excitement at every turn. Yet, it was beautiful.

Just like the ranch at the end of Winding Road.

The copy online about the family-owned-and-run establishment gave the bare-bones facts: over a hundred acres of land, residential housing on the property as well as a horse stable, barns and the Wild Iris Retreat, also owned and run by Nashes. Riley had done as much homework as she could to dig a little deeper, using Google Earth to zoom in on the land and get a general feel for it.

Trees, fields, mountains. The usual.

Yet, before Winding Road had even ended,

Riley had been stunned at the beauty surrounding them.

Rolling fields of green dipped and straightened around, between and at the edges of a forest that went across the ranch and seemingly all the way into town. Ranch buildings, including a red barn that looked like it belonged on a postcard, were interspersed in between, looking as natural as the scenery around them. Overlook was a shock of flora. Just as the mountains in the distance were. Riley had seen the curved outlines against the darkening blue sky when she'd first driven up to the party. She had had the strongest urge to reach out and pretend to touch them, tracing their dips and peaks like a child enthralled in a moment of wonder.

Now, at the very least, she understood some of her sister's reasoning for settling in Overlook.

It was a far cry from lives that had crumbled in the last year.

It was a cozy and beautiful respite.

But that didn't mean Riley was any more comfortable lying to everyone who reached out to say hello. One major drawback of the small town? Everyone seemed to know everyone else. She stuck out like a sore thumb. Even more so after her impromptu, and embarrassing, run-in with Desmond.

No sooner had she made it to the end of the tent, ready to glide over into the next one, did a man catch her attention. He was short, stocky and had hair that was messy but not in the charming way. His blazer hung a little too loosely on his frame and the shirt beneath it was somewhat wrinkled. His brown eyes jumped to her and then the area around them.

Riley might be nervous about pretending to be her sister but she had a feeling the man in front of her was a lot more nervous about something else.

"Pretty nice party, huh?" he greeted. "Desmond Nash sure is something, isn't he?"

Riley felt her sister's customer-service smile move across her lips.

Play the part.

"Yes! To both! I'm definitely impressed and having a great time."

The man's brows pulled in together for the briefest of moments. Riley didn't know how to classify the emotion that did it but then he was smiling again.

"You aren't the only one. I'm Brett." Riley expected him to offer his hand but he didn't move an inch.

"Jenna Stone."

"So how long have you been living in Overlook? I don't think I've seen you around."

Brett took a small step forward as if he was trying to physically engage with the conversation. It put him close enough that Riley could smell a hint of cologne. It wasn't altogether pleasant.

"Not long enough to know everyone yet," she

hedged. While Riley had been in Overlook for a little over a month, Jenna had made the move six months before that. Very few locals knew her by sight, let alone name. If Brett didn't recognize her then Riley wasn't about to give out information on her sister. "How about you?"

The man shrugged.

"Not that long either."

He didn't offer anything else. A silence moved between them. The piano medley faded out and was replaced by an acoustic guitar.

"Well," she finally broke in. "This party sure is great. Just like Second Wind. Desmond Nash really has a knack for knowing how to help people, doesn't he?"

Brett actually snorted.

"People like him always think they have the answers—I'll give you that."

Riley was starting to feel uncomfortable outside her lying. She didn't know this man—okay, *anyone* at the party—but she didn't think her sister would want to make a connection with him. Jenna was trying to grow her business in Overlook and Riley couldn't imagine Brett was into graphic design.

"This music is lovely, though, isn't it?" she asked lamely. The man wasn't taking any normal social cues in the conversation. He just kept staring. Eyes never straying from hers.

I've never felt more awkward in my life, Riley had the time to think.

She took an unintentional step backward. That, at least, he seemed to register. His smile widened. He nodded.

"It's sure something." He angled his body as if to leave. Instead he held out his arm. "Maybe we can dance to it?"

Riley felt like she was getting whiplash from the very brief and exceptionally strange conversation. She understood that not everyone could wear charm with ease—heck, her ex-husband Davies used to say she could burn through a good conversation with just one heated opinion in a flash—but there was something about the man that slunk under her skin and went to itching. Still, Riley tried to be gracious as she let him down.

She *was* pretending to be Jenna after all.

"I would but there's a few people I was hoping to talk to before I started in on the fun. Rain check?"

Brett shrugged. He dropped his arm, seemingly nonplussed.

"Suit yourself."

Then he walked off.

Just like that.

Riley stared after him a moment, dumbfounded. Even though she wanted to go to the main tent, she decided to turn around. She was almost disappointed when Desmond Nash was nowhere to be seen.

SECOND WIND FOUNDATION had spent its career finding and funding nonprofits that all seemed to focus on helping people after tragedy. That's what Jenna had surmised when she was stepping Riley through small talk all day, yet that wasn't what any of the guests were discussing when Riley infiltrated each of their groups.

Instead the conversations ran the gamut of brief facts and heavy gossip. Not all of it Riley could follow, but still, she nodded along with everyone else. While Jenna had taught her everything she knew about Overlook, Second Wind and Desmond Nash, there was apparently a lot she hadn't.

"I hope that Second Wind building isn't an eyesore. I already don't like how many trees they cut to clear the lot to build."

"How much money did they spend on this party? Where does it come from? Don't you think it's suspicious?"

"Did you hear about what happened to Madi last year? And what about Caleb a few years before? Talk about bad luck. This family is lousy with it."

"I heard Desmond only came back because he couldn't handle being away from his mom."

"Did you see his limp? Remember when he was a kid? It's gotten a lot better. Do you think he had surgery on it?"

"Is Desmond here alone? Maybe I can change that."

The last conversation was from a woman who

appeared to be a few years younger than Riley's thirty. She was done up in a short cocktail dress made entirely of sequins. When she spotted the cowboy across the main tent—which Riley was excited to say she'd finally made it to without running into Brett—the woman had actually re-adjusted her dress, pushing her breasts higher. That woman was one of three around Riley. The only one she had focused on meeting was Claire, the owner of the same-named coffee shop in town. She had been kind and inviting as Riley introduced herself as Jenna. She had even asked for a business card once Riley was done with her memorized spiel.

The woman now openly ogling the business-man hadn't been as accommodating. She'd barely met Riley's eye when the introductions started. There was even a bit of a sneer when Claire asked if Riley had talked to the host already and she admitted she had.

The party might have been celebrating Second Wind and the man behind it, but Riley was find-ing a lot of focus had found its way to Desmond's dating life. Riley couldn't deny she was just a bit curious about it too.

She was about to finally cave and ask a few questions herself when Desmond seemingly dis-appeared. The next half hour brought in a new wave of conversational topics about other citizens of Overlook. Riley was starting to feel a touch uncomfortable with getting the 411 on relative strangers when a text vibrated her phone. It was from Jenna.

You've been there over an hour. Officially shutting down Twin Trickery. Come on home. Made snickerdoodles.

"Well, it's been wonderful to meet you all," Riley said, stifling a chuckle. She discreetly put her phone back into her clutch and fished for her keys. "But I think I'm going to call it a night."

Jenna and Riley were emotional bakers through and through, just like their mother. Every problem had a baked-good answer. Stressed? Gooey brownies. Angry? Chocolate-chip cookies with sea salt. Feeling guilty? Snickerdoodles. The list went on and changed with their moods but it had always made their father laugh.

"No matter what happens, the house always smells wonderful," he'd said.

Riley was more than ready to benefit from her sister's most recent bout of emotion. It was just kismet that it synced up with the fact that Riley's feet were starting to get sore.

Claire and the rest said their goodbyes and Riley strutted out into the night air with more pep in her step than before. When Jenna had begged Riley to pretend to be her for just one night, Riley had thought she was crazy. They were identical, sure, but their personalities varied widely, love for baking excluded.

Yet, as Riley followed the lit garden path to the makeshift parking area, she felt an unfurling of pride in her chest.

She'd helped her sister, and after the year Jenna had, it felt good to get a win for her.

Riley held on to the good feeling and got into her Jeep with a little excited hop. Her mind went to the snickerdoodles and she flung her high heels into the passenger's seat with vigor. She gave the party in the distance one more long look. The tents were lit up and glowing, the music was soft yet far-reaching and the stars and moon were nothing but ethereal above it all.

The Nash family ranch was a fairy tale.

One Riley was surprised to already miss.

But this wasn't her life. She wasn't like her sister. Overlook was a pit stop on the way to *something* else.

She'd hang around long enough to get her feet back on the ground and help her sister do the same. Then she'd be gone.

Riley drove out of the parking area and onto the road that went through the heart of the ranch. She was curious about the other paths that branched off it going this way and that but kept on straight to Winding Road. Once she was through the ranch's main gate and on the two-lane road, she pressed Play on the CD player and started to rock out to the *Greatest Hits of the 80s*. Moonlit scenery flashed by on either side of the Jeep until the open fields turned to forests and the darkness between the road's shoulders thickened.

Riley bobbed her head to the music, tapped her foot against the floorboard to the beat and was fully prepared to belt out the opening to "Take on Me" by a-ha. She slowed her speed since streetlights were far apart and few in number.

However, as she opened her mouth to start singing, she realized the headlights that had been somewhat behind her belonged to a car that was in no way adhering to caution. In fact, it was gaining speed.

Riley gripped the steering wheel, the words to her song forgotten. Her stomach tightened but her mind tried to reassure her she was just imaging that the car had not only sped up, but was nearing her bumper.

But then the car went into the middle of the road. The relief made her shoulders relax. The idiot was going to pass her. Impatience, that was all.

Riley glanced over as the red Buick drew even with her. The lights were on inside the car.

That relief vanished.

It was Brett.

He was smiling as he jerked his wheel toward her. Riley didn't have any time to react.

The song's chorus started to build.

It didn't have a chance to finish before Riley was screaming.

Chapter Three

The Jeep was sky blue and always carried a faint scent of cinnamon within its cab. Riley had owned and driven it for ten years and, in all of that time, never figured out why that was. It had driven her ex-husband mad trying to solve the mystery, just as it frustrated him that no matter what air freshener or spray he used, the scent of cinnamon never went away. Riley had oddly come to love the smell. It was synonymous with the feeling of home, if she was being honest with herself. It put her at ease.

However, not even the faintest trace of cinnamon could stop the horror that shot through Riley the second Brett's car connected with hers.

"What are you doing?"

An awful scraping of metal against metal combined with Riley's scream. She struggled to keep the Jeep on the road. Dirt and rocks kicked up from the shoulder. Brett didn't seem to care. He maneuvered his car back to the middle of the road while Riley tried for the brakes.

If it had been an accident before, it surely wasn't now.

Brett was relentless as he swerved right back at her. This time Riley tried to avoid him. She hit the brakes but not before the back of his car collided with her driver's-side door with a sickening crunch and undeniable force.

Riley wasn't sure what happened next.

One second she had a death grip on the steering wheel. The next the world was chaos.

Awful sounds surrounded her. Glass shattered, metal warped. Something hit Riley's face. The feeling of gravity tugging her in the wrong direction was tangled in a burning sensation across her chest. On reflex she tried to touch the pain when the world around her stopped moving. Once her hand was off the steering wheel, though, her entire body shifted.

Riley yelled.

She realized then that she was upside down.

Her red curls were reaching for the crumpled roof of the Jeep. One of Jenna's dangling earrings slipped out of its place and *plink*ed against something that sounded like glass below her. Something mechanical whined in the distance. The *Greatest Hits of the 80s* had gone silent but the lights from the dash sent a faint glow out around her.

Riley had a moment of total confusion. It left her frozen.

But then she heard it. A car door shutting.

Then Riley remembered why she was upside down in the first place.

Brett.

"Oh my God."

She fumbled for the seat-belt buckle and hit the release without any more hesitation. The distance between her seat and the roof of the Jeep was a short journey. And a painful one. Her palms hit glass and twisted metal but saved her face. Her knees didn't fare as well. Neither did her side. Pain radiated across her and settled in the injuries she had no time to investigate.

The driver's-side door was twisted and broken. Riley didn't need the full light of day to see she wasn't getting out that way. Instead she rolled over to the passenger's-side door. It was already hanging open.

Riley crawled for it like her life depended on it.

And, didn't it? All she could picture was Brett smiling.

He'd done this on purpose and that thought terrified Riley to the point of shaking as she pushed through the door and tumbled out of the Jeep and onto the grass.

She was on the shoulder where it dipped and disappeared into the start of the tree line.

It was that tree line she was scrambling for when Brett appeared next to the Jeep.

He was still smiling.

And he was holding a baseball bat.

Riley's heartbeat was in her ears. Her bare feet complained as she ran full tilt into the darkness of the woods. That run turned into a fast limp. She slapped tree trunks as she tried to navigate around them. Roots she couldn't see twisted the ground. Her feet caught them and the ground caught her body after. The beautiful dress she'd worried about getting dirty earlier that night was slowly becoming ribbons the farther into the trees she went.

The beauty of the moonlight and stars meant nothing. All she could think about was how no one knew where she was, how she'd not even looked for her phone before running and how that running was about to end. Her body couldn't keep it up. Not anymore.

So when she tripped over a fallen log, instead of getting up and keeping forward, Riley crawled along its length, kept low and hurried to a neighboring tree. She flattened herself against its trunk and prayed that Brett hadn't followed her.

"Here, kitty, kitty!"

Riley's stomach dropped somewhere near her feet. Brett's baritone carried with ease to where she was hiding. He *had* followed her. What's more, he'd kept up.

"You're fast. I'll give you that," he continued. There was a laboring effort to his words. He seemed, at least, tired by their jaunt through the woods so far. "But I'm guessing you're sitting still now. It's gonna be hard to get back up."

Riley was absolutely trembling but she was also weighing her options. She could keep hiding and hope he just left or she could try to make it back to the Jeep. There was no telling where the woods ended. She didn't want to find out by running all night into the darkness that the trees kept going for miles and miles.

"I just want to talk," Brett said after a moment. Riley almost sang in relief. He sounded farther away from her. "Come on out!"

Riley took a deep breath. She thought about her sister. She thought about Hartley. She thought about her parents, and she hated to realize, she thought about her ex-husband Davies.

If he hadn't lied, I wouldn't be here right now.

But, the fact was, she *was* there and if she wanted to see her sister and nephew again, she was going to have to move like Hell was on her tail.

Riley didn't waste any more time. She hiked up her dress, pushed off the ground and prayed Brett wouldn't hear her.

If she could get back to the road she could—

Two arms wrapped around her no more than a foot from her hiding place.

They were strong and unmoving, a vise keeping her against him, pinning her arms to her sides. When a hand slapped over her mouth, Riley had every intention of biting through the bone if she had to.

"Quiet or he'll hear us."

The smooth, deep voice most certainly didn't belong to Brett. Riley craned her neck around to see who had her back against his chest.

Riley didn't have enough emotion left in her to be surprised that it was Desmond Nash. Wearing his cowboy hat to boot.

"DON'T MAKE A SOUND," Desmond whispered at Jenna's ear. She nodded. He felt the movement across his body. Just as he felt her trembling.

He knew he wasn't faring much better. He'd been running after the man and her since he saw them take off into the woods. Even without his limp it had been in no way an easy trek.

Slowly he took his hand from her mouth. He loosened his arms around her but didn't fully disengage. Instead he lowered his lips so close to her ear that she jumped when he spoke.

"Does he have a gun?"

Her shrug moved his arms.

"All I saw was a baseball bat."

Desmond's blood would have been boiling at that if he hadn't been trying to stay focused. He let go of her and reached into the pocket of his slacks. He yanked his cell phone out, careful to hide the light of his screen. He'd pulled them behind a tree but he didn't know exactly where the man was.

Desmond turned Jenna around and handed her the phone. He leaned in again so close that their foreheads touched.

"My brother is on the phone," he said, barely above a whisper. "Talk to him while I talk to that man. Do you know who he is?"

The screen's glow showed Desmond the dark eyes he'd admired over an hour ago. They widened. Desmond wanted to give her more comfort but he could hear her pursuer stomping around, crunching through the underbrush. He was starting to swear.

He was losing patience.

Desperate men did desperate things and Desmond wasn't going to wait to see if this man had any last-ditch efforts he was ready to employ to get Jenna.

Her voice wavered but she managed an answer.

"He was at the party. His name is Brett."

Desmond scrolled through the list of people he knew named Brett as he nodded to her. When he stepped around the tree, he was sure he hadn't talked to anyone with that name during the party. A troubling fact but one of many that had and was taking place.

The moonlight barely scratched the darkness's surface but Desmond's vision had adjusted enough to see the outline of the man. He was a few yards away, slinking between standing and downed trees. The bat was propped up on his shoulder.

He was looking for Jenna.

He was about to find Desmond instead.

Desmond had moved around in a semicircle so that Jenna wasn't behind him. He didn't want to chance her getting hurt if there was cross fire. Desmond also wasn't going to let her attacker get away. Brett might have pulled up after the wreck and looked like a man wanting to help but him chasing Jenna into the woods when Desmond arrived had painted a damning picture of intentions. The woods they were in stretched back for miles, ultimately leading to a neighboring property. Through that you could get back to the Nash family ranch.

Another chance Desmond wasn't going to take.

If he could just keep the man occupied while he waited for Declan and Caleb to arrive…

"I have a gun. You move—I shoot."

Desmond's voice echoed around them.

Brett stopped.

For a moment no one spoke.

Desmond wasn't bluffing about the gun. He had one. Just not with him. He hadn't brought it to the gala, and when he sneaked out of the gala to go to the construction site, he hadn't thought to go by the house and get it. Still, Brett didn't have a light. They were both dealing in outlines and shadows. He wouldn't be able to see that Desmond wasn't holding a gun.

Then again, the same could be said for Desmond. The man might have been wielding a bat but that didn't mean he wasn't also carrying something else.

"There was a car accident," Brett said. There was concern clear in his voice. Along with surprise. "I tried to help the woman who was in it but she ran in here. I think something's wrong with her."

"Did you call the police?" Desmond stalled.

There was no response.

Desmond narrowed his eyes, locking in on the outline in the distance.

"Why do you have a bat?" he added.

The outline shifted. Desmond balled his fists.

"You've gone quiet, friend," Desmond said after another tense silence. "Why don't you tell me why you're really out here?"

A flurry of motion streaked straight toward him. Desmond stood his ground, careful not to blink. The man was coming right at him, bat raised and growling like a deranged animal.

It wasn't the time, it wasn't the place and it certainly wasn't the same Desmond but just like that he was back in a memory. The worst memory.

He was eight. The smell of summer was dancing along the heat and humidity and creating the need for the Nash triplets to do something other than hang around the ranch, and when the park called their name, they answered.

Desmond remembered their laughter as they played hide-and-seek. He also remembered Madi's screams.

The man, one he still saw in his dreams from time to time, had been a walking nightmare then. Yet, after he'd hurt Madi and after he'd hurt Caleb, all he had been to the Desmond of then was a target.

A target for his anger. For his fear. For his confusion.

Without a second thought Desmond had gone at a man twice his size. A man who had a gun. A man who had a plan he didn't understand.

Just as the man with the bat was doing now.

The dull pain in Desmond's leg reminded him of how raw emotions could irrevocably change the outcome for the worst.

Brett was acting on instinct.

Desmond was acting on patience.

Brett let out a wild war cry as the space between them disappeared. He wound the bat and his arm up, pulling it back over his shoulder, and prepared to swing. Desmond didn't need lights surrounding them to know where to hit first.

He waited until the last possible second and lunged at the man.

They exchanged grunts as Desmond's shoulder made contact with Brett's chest. The attack wasn't meant to put the man out of commission. It was meant to stun him.

And boy did it work.

His momentum redirected to the ground. Desmond fell with him.

As soon as they hit, Desmond made fast work of grabbing for the bat.

Brett growled, once again sounding more animal than human. He didn't relinquish the bat without a fight. The man punched out with his left fist. It connected, but so did Desmond's flurry of hits in return.

Their scuffle turned into a rolling match as each tried to get the upper hand.

Desmond held on to the bat just as Brett did, neither relinquishing control.

It wasn't until a light appeared a few feet from them that Brett's attention broke. Desmond leaned into the oversight. He pulled the bat free, delivered a hard blow with his fist against the man's jaw and watched with deep satisfaction as the body he'd been fighting went slack. Brett thumped back to the ground. Desmond took a deep breath and pushed up and away from him, brandishing the bat over his shoulder.

With a heaving chest, bruised jaw and a layer of dirt and sweat galore, he turned to the light expecting to see his brothers.

What he saw instead were two dark eyes and wild red hair.

"I didn't want to leave you," Jenna said. She motioned to something in her other hand. It was a stick. "I was going to try to hit him." She gave a weak laugh.

Then her face fell.

Now that they weren't trying to hide the cell phone's light, Desmond could see more of the woman.

Including the tears starting to run down her cheeks.

Desmond closed the space between them just in time for the woman to fall into his arms.

They were still standing like that when the sheriff arrived.

Chapter Four

Lights danced between the trees as the woods filled with men and women dressed to the nines. The sheriff was still in his suit from the gala, same as Detective Nash who ran into the woods alongside his brother. A woman wearing a beautiful velvet green gown that shimmered in the glow of the cell phones and flashlights brought up the rear with a look as severe as the other two.

All three had their guns drawn.

When they saw Desmond standing there and Brett unconscious on the ground, Riley could nearly feel their relief.

"I'm okay. He just got a few lucky hits in is all," Desmond assured the sheriff before he could ask it. Then everyone's gaze fell to Riley. She was still against Desmond's chest, head turned like a terrified child peeking out around the skirt of her mother. Though the warmth of Desmond's embrace in no way reminded her of her mother.

Riley opened her mouth to say *something* but the words got caught in her throat. Her body had already devolved into a shaking mess. She didn't say it but she had a sneaking suspicion that Desmond's hold on her was the only thing keeping her upright. Thankfully, he also spoke for her.

"We need to get her to the hospital."

"EMTs are on the way," the woman said. She followed Desmond's brother to Brett. He pulled out a set of cuffs from his jacket pocket and she covered him while he tugged Brett's arms behind his back and closed the metal around his wrists. The sheriff holstered his gun. His expression softened as he looked at Riley.

"I'm Declan. I was the one on the phone," he said, tapping the badge on his hip that said Sheriff. Claire had already pointed out the sheriff and the detective at the gala, but even if Riley hadn't known about the man, she would have guessed it right away. Declan Nash was giving off pure authority just by standing still. "What's your name?"

Despite everything that had just happened, despite the fact that she was talking to the sheriff, Riley felt the irrational urge to stick to the lie she'd been telling all night. To protect her sister from scrutiny. It was weirdly easy to keep it going now.

"Jenna. Jenna Stone."

No recognition flashed across the sheriff's expression. Neither did suspicion. He simply nodded.

"Well, Jenna, how do you want to do this?

Would you like to wait for the EMTs to come in or do you think you're up for walking back to the road?" He motioned to the woman. "Detective Santiago *and* Desmond will be with you every step of the way while Detective Nash and I wait here for backup."

"I can carry you, if you need," Desmond offered. His words rumbled through his chest and against her body. It was encouraging in a way. She took a deep breath, steadying her nerves.

She was safe now.

They both were.

"I can walk," she decided. "I don't want to be out here anymore."

The sheriff nodded.

"I don't blame you one bit on that. I'll come talk to you after we get everything handled here." He shared a look with Desmond. "And you're okay to walk too?"

"Yeah. The leg has been through a lot worse."

Slowly he released his hold on Riley, as if afraid she'd fall to pieces once he wasn't keeping her together anymore. Riley hated to admit it but she was worried about the same thing.

But then the warmth of him was gone, replaced by an ominous chill in the night air. Detective Santiago walked up to her side. Her gun was lowered but she didn't put it away.

Riley didn't look back at Brett, lying motionless on the ground.

She also didn't dare look down at the baseball bat discarded at Desmond's feet.

The EMTs were already at the road by the time they came out of the tree line. So was a growing crowd. It was as if every gala attendee had decided to ditch their vehicles for a better view. Uniformed deputies were arriving and trying to block off the road. Brett had left his car on the shoulder opposite the Jeep.

The poor Jeep.

It was upside down and resembled a crushed Coke can.

Riley sniffled back tears again as she walked past it to the back of the waiting ambulance.

The EMT was a woman who looked around Riley's age and obviously knew Desmond. She gave him a once-over and told him she was glad he was okay before turning her attention to Riley. The once-over came with a look of acute concern, followed by a recommendation that they go to the hospital. It created a new surge of panic. She must have read it in Riley's face. Her expression softened.

"Everything looks like superficial wounds but it's better to be safe than sorry." She pointed to the Jeep. "You were in that when it flipped, I'm assuming?"

"I was."

The EMT gave an apologetic smile.

"Then I think we should get you checked out. Just to make sure you're alright. Okay?"

Riley conceded and soon she was sitting on the gurney. Detective Santiago joined her, taking the side seat and producing a notepad out of her purse. The shoulder holster she had on was quite the contrast to her gown. She asked questions and Riley answered them the best she could while being caught up in the bustle of the EMT and the driver. So much so that she didn't notice when Desmond slipped away. He didn't come back and soon they were on the road and pointed to Overlook Hospital.

Riley tried not to look for the cowboy who had saved her. Or feel the sting that he had disappeared without a word.

THE HOSPITAL FLUORESCENTS were in no way flattering. Not that Riley had a chance of looking anything other than *rough*. She stood in front of the bathroom mirror and tried to decide what looked the worst.

Was it the darkening bruise across her cheek from, she assumed, the airbag deploying? Or maybe the small cuts along her forehead from glass? Maybe it was the fact that all of her makeup had streaked down her face when she lost it and sobbed into a relative stranger's shirt.

It would have been the state of Jenna's dress had she still been wearing it. A once beautiful and daring piece had been torn in several places, including a thick tear over her hip. She'd seen her lacy black underwear through it the moment she'd stepped into the ER lobby. Now she was in a hospital gown, wearing safety socks that were hiding bandages for her poor feet. Like her purse and phone, she'd forgotten her shoes in the Jeep. There were other little cuts and bruises across her body that would probably make onlookers do a double take, but thankfully, no injuries extended past minor aches and pains.

Still, she had been glad for Detective Santiago's presence as she waited for the nurse to take her to get X-rays. Once everything had calmed down, Riley realized her neck was throbbing—because her nerves were officially shot. It didn't help that she spent the time between recounting what had happened on Winding Road and at the gala with Brett. Neither woman could think of a reason for his actions but the detective promised they'd get to the bottom of it.

Now, alone in the bathroom attached to the small room she'd been assigned, Riley decided to stop dwelling on her appearance. After the night she'd had, she was just thankful to be alive.

A knock sounded against the room door. Riley gave herself a nod of reassurance in the mirror and went out of the bathroom and back to the bed. The movements made her wince. Her feet were still tender from running through the woods.

"Come in," she called once she was back in bed. She positioned the blanket over her lap, self-conscious about her mostly bare legs.

Desmond Nash appeared around the door, sans cowboy hat. He did, however, have a purse in his hands and a smile on his face.

"Sorry I didn't get this here sooner," he greeted. "My truck got blocked in and then Declan got blocked in and, well, let's just say Winding Road wasn't made to handle fifty-plus gawkers, their cars and an active investigation."

What had been long strides at the gala had now become a noticeable limp as Desmond brought her purse over. Riley had assumed the limp she'd witnessed in the woods was due to an injury from the fight but now she wondered if it was from an older one instead.

Either way, she wasn't about to pry. Not when she was filled with equal amounts gratitude and guilt. She addressed the first feeling with her own smile and open arms for her bag.

"Thank you so much for getting this," she said, sincere. "I forgot about even trying to find my phone or purse until I was in here already. Thank you!"

Riley could have cried for joy. She hadn't remembered where her phone was before the crash. Now she found it within the folds of faux leather.

There were five missed calls. All were from Jenna.

Riley felt that second emotion bubbling to the surface.

Guilt.

She had convinced herself to wait until the doctor officially said Riley could leave before calling Jenna. But really it had been more about keeping herself sane. She knew the moment she saw Jenna, the emotional dam would break again. Just like it had in the woods with Desmond.

Now, though, Riley knew she had to face the music. She didn't want her sister to worry more than she had to, but first, Riley had to address the other well of guilt within her.

Desmond was studying her, his brows drawn together in thought.

"Are you okay?" he asked, simply.

"Yeah. It all looks much worse than it is."

"I heard you got some X-rays done?"

She nodded.

"My neck was hurting but they said it was just the whiplash." Riley felt the heat of a blush before she continued. "Now I'm just waiting to make sure I don't have a bad reaction to the pain meds they gave me. It was a, uh, shot."

Right in the butt cheek, she thought but definitely didn't say out loud.

"I already feel a lot better," she added. "I'm just tired now."

"Good," Desmond said. "That's good."

"What about you?" She traced the mark across

his jawline. She hadn't been able to see the punches being thrown in the woods but she'd heard the hits landing.

Desmond shrugged.

"Nothing a bag of frozen peas can't help. It coulda been worse."

"I know the feeling. If you hadn't been driving by when you did—" Riley didn't need to finish the thought. She knew later she'd cycle through the several what-if situations and go back into panic mode. She didn't want that now. "What I mean to say is thank you. And not just for grabbing my purse."

Desmond Nash sure could smile. Even the small stretch was quite the sight. So, when it snuffed out so suddenly, Riley felt a different kind of panic.

"I'm sorry that it even happened in the first place," he said with startling venom. "The gala was meant to be a happy occasion and yet you were stalked by a guest. I'm sorry, Jenna. I really am."

Riley felt the burn in her cheeks. Time to address the other reason for her guilt.

"I in no way blame you for Brett," she started. "*But* I do need to apologize to *you*."

Desmond's eyebrow rose.

"I'm not *actually* Jenna Stone."

DESMOND HADN'T SEEN that one coming.

Jenna—or, well, maybe not—let her gaze hit

the floor before she dragged it back up to his. Her cheeks had tinted crimson. When she continued her voice had lowered.

"I'm Riley Stone, her sister."

Desmond liked to think he was a fair guy. After what his family had been through, he had made a life out of striving to do what was right by his loved ones and the people he met through his philanthropy. Those goals had always gone hand in hand with being a straight shooter. There wasn't room for lies or deceit in his life.

Not after that day in the park when he was eight.

Not after the three days in that basement.

Not after the repercussions of it spread out and consumed his father years later.

The truth, *honesty*, was important to him.

Important to living a life he hoped to never get as complicated as it had before, a goal all of his family had been trying to attain with varying degrees of success.

So, despite the trauma that had just happened to the woman, Desmond's default response went from confusion to deep suspicion to, quite frankly, disappointment.

Also it highlighted one concrete fact Desmond had somehow managed to ignore until that moment given what they'd been through.

He knew nothing about the woman sitting in front of him.

It was a rare occurrence in Overlook, one he should have looked into before rushing over to the hospital to make sure she was okay.

"I can explain," Riley hurried to tack on, her cheeks turning an even deeper shade of crimson. It contrasted against her pale skin, making her freckles stand out even more. "See, my sister, Jenna, started her own business a while back and really put herself out there to do it, and tonight was supposed to be her chance to finally connect with the local businesses and leaders of the community. *But* then Hartley, her son, wasn't feeling good and she panicked and decided to stay home. She was so worried that if she didn't go people would judge her for being a single mom and not give her a chance to prove herself and so I decided to go in her place." She let out a long breath, deflating.

"But you told Declan, the sheriff, you were Jenna," he pointed out.

She gave him an apologetic shrug.

"There was so much going on and I—I don't know, in my mind I was protecting her image still."

Desmond understood loyalty but it didn't take away from the fact that she'd lied to *his* family, law enforcement.

"This could change the entire investigation. If the attack wasn't random or because of opportunity, then Brett clearly knew he was targeting you, not your sister. How did you not think this was going to change everything? How irresponsible can you be?"

Desmond started to get hot under the collar. And not because Riley was as beautiful out of her makeup as she was glammed up. He'd nicknamed her the siren at the party and here she was, admitting she'd led him and law enforcement astray.

All at once Desmond couldn't help but think of anything other than his father. He'd run his life into the ground trying to solve the mystery of what had happened to the Nash triplets and eventually died because of it. Among the stress that had done him in? People lying and hindering his investigation.

Logically, Desmond knew it wasn't the same situation, yet a wounded heart doesn't always accept logic.

"How did you even think this was going to pan out? Don't you think people would have noticed that the woman they met at the party wasn't the same woman when Jenna came by? We may be a small town but we aren't small-minded."

Riley opened her mouth to say something—what could she really say though that would quell his rising frustration?—when a shout from the hallway drew their attention. The door opened behind them. Jasmine "Jazz" Santiago, Caleb's partner and best friend, gave him a look he couldn't quite place.

"Uh, Jenna? I think someone is looking for you."

Riley didn't correct her as she jumped up and padded by them and out the door. Desmond followed, ready to make the woman admit she'd lied about her identity, when he saw the point of confusion Jazz had latched on to.

"Oh my God," a woman yelled at the sight of Riley. She was at the end of the hallway, a toddler on her hip.

Riley's entire demeanor changed. She let out a cry that instantly turned to tears. Both women ran through the distance between them until they collided in an embrace in the middle of the hallway.

"I knew it," the other woman cried out. "I knew something was wrong. I *felt* it!"

She buried her head in Riley's dark red curls, her own dark red curls matching perfectly.

All at once Desmond realized why the switch had been brilliant.

"They're twins."

Chapter Five

The lights in the kitchen were warm and inviting.

Riley was so tired she felt like languishing on the floor beneath them if that meant she could get some peace. No matter how brief.

Jenna, on the other hand, was not in the mood to let Riley get off that easily. Since the embrace at the hospital two hours earlier, she hadn't left Riley's side. Not even when she'd had to go to the restroom after downing a full bottle of water.

"Next time I get chased down by a madman that no one seems to know and look like I've been put in a blender, we'll see how you handle it," she'd said when Riley had complained.

Not that Riley was surprised. In fact, she wasn't even upset. After what her sister had been through in the last year, she knew Jenna was even more determined to protect what was left of her life. And Jenna was fiercely rooted in the belief that her twin was under that purview.

Now, looking wistfully where Jenna was standing in the kitchen, with both hands on her hips, Riley knew she was about to receive an earful.

"Do you know that I had to run past the hospital guard *and* go around yelling before they could finally calm me down enough to direct me," she said, voice low but still throbbing with anger. Hartley had been asleep since they'd been given the green light to leave by the doctor and the sheriff. Riley had expected to be kept longer once she'd pulled the sheriff aside and admitted she'd given him the wrong name but neither he nor Desmond had berated her—at least not for a second time—or pulled out the cuffs and read her her rights. Instead Riley had been told to go to the sheriff's department first thing in the morning so they could sort everything out.

"I said I was sorry already," Riley tried. "I was going to call you when I got released. I didn't want you to worry."

"Worry? *Worry?*" Jenna placed her hand against her chest. "There I was just making your favorite cookies and I *felt* it, Riley. Right here in my chest. I was so sure that something happened to you that, when you didn't answer your phone, I drove out to the ranch, fully prepared to hunt you down. But I never got there, did I, Riley? Why is that?"

This part Riley had been briefed on earlier. Still, she repeated the answer.

"Because you got stopped at the roadblock…

Where you saw the Jeep flipped over on the side of the road."

Jenna nodded with angry enthusiasm.

"When no one could tell me if you were alright after *being taken by ambulance* to the hospital, I had to drive there with a three-year-old and honest-to-God fear in my soul all because you didn't want to worry me by calling."

At the last part Jenna's voice broke. Like Riley she'd nearly sobbed when they'd first seen each other. Now her eyes were as swollen as Riley's. Still, they rimmed with tears.

"Next time—though there better not *be* a next time—you call, Riley. Plain and simple. You. Call."

Riley nodded.

"I promise, Jen, I will."

Seemingly satisfied, Jenna gave her sister one more long embrace before shaking herself and moving to the pantry. She pulled out a festive container and set it down on the countertop.

"Now it's time we finally had some snickerdoodles then."

Riley's exhaustion was replaced by acute hunger for the cookies. Jenna had only eaten one by the time Riley had consumed three.

IT WAS ALMOST three in the morning when Riley finally settled into bed. Jenna's house was small yet cozy, including the two bedrooms. Hartley slept on a bed in Jenna's room while Riley was tucked against a full-size mattress that almost took up the entire room. It was a far cry from the massive house Jenna had resided in with her ex-husband over a year ago but Riley couldn't help but love the small home much more.

Its walls were filled with memories; its space filled with knickknacks, decorations and furniture all carrying sentimental value and function to Jenna's and Hartley's lives. It wasn't cold. It wasn't void of feeling. It wasn't a prison.

Jenna had downgraded in space, sure, but she'd more than upgraded in warmth.

Riley lay on her back and stared at the ceiling fan she'd helped Jenna install after it had been Riley's turn to downgrade and move in. They'd fought after Jenna had dropped a screw and then Riley had dropped the screwdriver. Hartley, ever curious, had cried from his gated play area because he couldn't grab either item and put it in his mouth. It had been a disastrous half-hour ordeal and yet there the fan was. They had made it work. Now it was a part of the house's story. A memory that was ingrained in its fabric.

An ache of sentimentality cracked open in Riley's chest. Loneliness and loss reverberated through those cracks. She rolled onto her side, wincing at the shot's injection site, and let out a long, body-sagging breath against the pillow.

Riley thought about Davies, about Jenna, about

the jobs she and her sister had both loved and had to give up, about the malicious Brett and then about the prepossessing Desmond Nash.

Claiming to know Desmond was foolish. However, seeing the disappointment and then hearing the anger at her lie?

That had been somewhat painful.

Less than a year ago life had been simpler.

Now it was proving to hurt more often than not.

"WHAT'S THE SAYING? All press is good press?"

Caleb took off his blazer and flung it over the dining-room chair. His detective's badge was still hanging around his neck. Declan had opted to go to the department instead of calling it a night like the rest of them. It *was* almost four in the morning. The sheriff was dedicated to a fault.

"*Any* press is good press 'as long as they spell my name right,'" Desmond corrected. He scrubbed his hand down his face.

Caleb chuckled.

"Well, as much as we're in the paper I'm sure they'll get your name right." Caleb was trying to lighten the mood, something he'd been attempting more since he'd met his wife, Nina. Her optimism, coupled with their mother's fierce belief that you should try any and everything to remain as stress-free as possible, had turned many scowls and silence from the man into teasing jokes and grins.

It was a good look for Caleb but not one Desmond particularly cared for at the moment.

"A bonus to opening Second Wind here in Overlook was to give the residents something positive to associate with our names," he said. "Not just another insane story about some crazy person seeking vengeance or someone with a penchant for senseless violence."

Caleb sighed. He pulled a chair out and fell into it. Desmond dropped into the one opposite. They both took a second to glance at the chair at the head of the table. Sometimes when it was just the two of them together, the urge to look for Madi turned into them physically doing it even when they knew exactly where she was. Their mother called the phenomenon just another piece of their triplet connection.

"As senseless as what happened was, it didn't happen to any of us Nashes," Caleb started. "And just because Ms. Stone was coming from your party doesn't mean it was your fault that she was attacked. Hell, Des, there's no telling what would have happened had you not been there to help. Yeah, the press might bring up all the madness we've been through in the last few years and yeah, maybe even recap—well, *that*, but all they're going to say about you is that you helped make an unfortunate situation a lot better. You might get a little more popular over the next week or two but construction on Second Wind will continue, you'll go back to work and eventually it'll just be another story recirculating in the gossip mill. Okay?"

Desmond nodded. He knew his brother was right. The gala had been open to the public. There had been no screening of the guests and no way for them to know that Brett had intended to do what he had. Or, apparently, who Brett even was. Once Desmond was able to see the man in the light, he confirmed to Declan that he'd never seen the man. In fact, none of the Nashes had recognized him or the name.

"Don't worry. We'll get to the bottom of who he is and why this Brett attacked Riley when we talk to him later today," Caleb added on, sensing his brother's concern. "Men like him like talking. All we have to do is wait and listen."

"It's times like these I wouldn't mind being in law enforcement," Desmond admitted. He smirked, actively trying to loosen the tension in his shoulders. "Can't you and Declan bend the rules and let me in on an interrogation?"

Caleb chuckled.

"I'd like to be a fly on the wall for that request. Maybe if we weren't fraternal we could just switch."

Desmond had a feeling his brother had been waiting to loop back to the fact that Riley and Jenna were twins since he'd found out at the hospital. There was a slight childlike wonder in his eyes. None of the Nash triplets had ever met a set of identical twins. Under different circumstances it would have been more intriguing to Desmond, he was sure.

"It was like seeing someone staring into a mirror," he had to admit. "Madi would have flipped. Hell, it had me speechless for a second. I still can't believe they tried to pull that crap."

Like someone had flipped a switch, the mood changed in the little dining room. Caleb slid into his detective's face, as Desmond had called it through the years. He was on a case. He was looking for clues. He was coming to conclusions.

He was staring at Desmond.

"Two hours," Caleb finally said. Desmond felt his brow rise in question.

"Two hours?"

"That's how long Riley's lie lasted. Only two hours. Remember that the next time you see her. Maybe remind that serious face of yours to calm down." Caleb pushed the chair back and stood. He had spent a good amount of his career hiding the exhaustion that sometimes went with a long day or night but now Desmond saw the drag of it pulling down his shoulders. If he didn't live on the ranch too, no more than five minutes down the road, Desmond would have told him to stay. As it stood, Desmond pulled himself up and walked his brother to the door. Caleb slowed down to make up for his limp.

"I'm fine," Desmond said before Caleb could ask about his leg. "Nothing some pain meds and a few hours of sleep won't fix."

"Good. Just don't let Ma see you doing that pained face tomorrow. We had to move heaven and earth to keep her from leaving the ranch tonight. Madi said she thought she was going to have to get Julian to tackle her at one point to keep her from rushing to the hospital."

"For a woman who preaches doing everything in her power to be stress-free, she sure soaks it up when it's out there."

"Well, when you have kids as awesome as us, can you blame her for being worried?"

Desmond snorted.

"Calling yourself awesome doesn't make it so," he said.

"Agree to disagree, Des. Agree. To. Disagree."

Caleb clapped him on the shoulder and then bounded down the porch steps toward his truck. The main house stood a hundred or so yards away, lights off. The Nash children had grown up in that house and now their mother lived there alone.

Long before Desmond had agreed to bring Second Wind to Overlook—or even had Second Wind as a thought in his head—he'd built his house close to the main one on purpose. He didn't want to live in his childhood home but he also didn't want to leave his mother by herself.

Even though he'd barely spent time in Overlook, he felt comforted by the fact that all she had to do was look out her window and see the house there. Now that he was living there full-time, Desmond saw how it could be tricky being so close to his mother. While he had made peace with the fact that he'd have his limp for the remainder of his life, he had a sneaking suspicion his mother still had a hard time seeing it from time to time.

Desmond took a deep breath. The chill that had spread across Overlook filled his lungs. He hoped in the next few hours it would stay. He was no stranger to sweat-inducing heat and humidity— you wouldn't hear *him* complaining about it— but he had to admit he enjoyed cooler weather. In fact, before the gala had started, he'd found himself staring at the mountains in the distance and hoping for snow.

Now the gala felt like days ago, not hours.

Desmond moved back into the house and straight for the shower. He tried to clear his head as hot water beat against his back and aching leg.

Yet, his thoughts wandered to tangles of dark red hair.

Two hours.

That's how long the lie had lasted.

Desmond knew his frustration was an overreaction, but there wasn't anything he could do about it now.

He got out of the shower, dried off, slipped on a pair of boxers and fell into bed.

It wasn't until he was dozing off that the reason for him being on Winding Road in the first place when he saw Riley and Brett made noise in his thoughts.

After Caleb had also tried to push off telling him what the graffiti on Second Wind's construction site had said, Desmond had sneaked away to see it for himself.

It had ruined his night with one look. If it hadn't been for the excitement that followed, Desmond had no doubt he would have focused on that for the remainder of the party.

Now the overtly stylized sentence he'd seen spray painted floated behind dozing eyes.

"Can't even win a simple game of hide-and-seek."

Chapter Six

Two weeks went by and the media didn't let a day pass without some mention of what had happened after the Second Wind gala.

Brett had been identified as Brett Calder, a man no one seemed to know personally in town. A newspaper article stated that he had a history of domestic violence and ties to an up-and-coming criminal group out of the city of Kilwin. As far as the attack on Riley Stone, it was one of opportunity. There was no rhyme or reason past that, according to his own admission of guilt. He had seen her leave, alone, and followed.

Desmond Nash, famed local businessman, had been in the right place at the right time. Another story in the form of a social media post for an online publication questioned why Desmond was out on the road during his party in the first place and wondered at his motives, as well as his involvement. A poorly Photoshopped picture was posted in the comments and showed a younger Desmond in a group picture with a younger Brett.

The writer called it a conspiracy. That comment was eventually deleted, along with the account that had posted it.

A few other county newspapers and TV stations picked up the story but not for the sheer audacity of Brett Calder's attack. Instead it was blatantly obvious that everyone's interest revolved around Desmond's involvement. Some stories didn't just stop with him. They reported on and recapped earlier news stories about the attacks on Caleb and his wife two years ago and Madeline's wrongly accused involvement in a homicide the year before. Two stories even included the infamous Nash triplet abduction, the greatest unsolved mystery in Overlook's history.

Riley had known that Desmond and his family had lived through trauma; he was very open about that and his intentions of helping others like him through Second Wind, but she didn't know the gritty details that went along with it. She had felt a flare of shame as she'd read a social media post that listed bullet points of facts.

The eight-year-old triplets had sneaked out to a local park.

They'd been playing a game of hide-and-seek when a man with a gun had grabbed Madeline Nash.

Trying to help her, Caleb Nash had been shot in the shoulder and Desmond Nash had had his leg broken by their attacker.

Using the unconscious Madeline as incentive to do as he said, the man took all three to an undisclosed cabin in the woods where the children were kept in the basement for three days.

They finally managed to escape by pretending that Desmond had stopped breathing and overpowering their abductor by working together when he came to check on the boy.

From there they ran through the woods until they found help. By the time authorities made it back to the cabin, their abductor was gone.

To this day no one had any information on the man or why he had done what he did, despite the triplets' father and then detective, Michael Nash, working the case hard until the day he died of a heart attack years later.

The story pulled at Riley's heartstrings, but it also made her angry. The family had already been through way more than most. People were just dredging up the old stories for shock value and clicks. A thought that was admonished by an opinion editorial in the local newspaper, the *Overlook Explorer.*

The op-ed was written by the current news editor, Delores Dearborn. In it she reminded the community that the Nash family did a lot for the town. She highlighted the sheriff's career as well as Caleb's time as a deputy and detective, pointed out that Dorothy Nash, their mother, had been an upstanding and valued resident of Overlook longer than most had been alive, reminded them of Madeline Nash's continued involvement in the community and wrapped the piece up with the bold statement that the Nash family had helped shape the town of Overlook just as much as the founding families if not more.

"Without the Nash family and their beloved ranch, who would we even be as a town? Not the Overlook I've come to know and love, that's for sure."

Delores had ended the article with a call to action. Give the Nash family the respect and privacy they deserve. Look to the future, instead, with the same excitement and vigor they've been using to dredge up the past.

It had been a wonderful and inspiring read. One that had resonated with Jenna also after they'd finally bought a copy. She put the newspaper down on the jungle gym's platform between them and blew out a long breath.

"I guess what they say is true," she said. "'Be kind because everyone is fighting their own battle.'"

It was a beautiful Saturday morning in Overlook. Sun shining, sixty degrees and they were visiting a kid-friendly park just off Main Street that Riley was excited to explore with her nephew. She had her hair pulled back in a low ponytail, was wearing a purposefully oversize T-shirt and had donned her sister's spandex running pants since half of Riley's clothes were still in boxes in the garage.

Jenna, on the other hand, was wearing a no-nonsense business outfit, complete with a slick black portfolio in one hand. She kept glancing in the direction of Main Street and Claire's Café.

"Just go," Riley finally said. "Claire took this meeting already knowing about the switch. She was a single mom for years. She said she understood why we did it."

Jenna looked unsure.

"What if she just wants to ask me about what happened to you? Or just wants to get mad at me in person for attempting to lie to everyone?"

Hartley let out a trill of laughter as he slapped one of the colorful spinners in the wall of the jungle gym set. Riley couldn't help but smile.

"Listen, I have my phone. If she does anything crazy or mean just send an SOS text and me and the munchkin will come running. Okay? Now *go*."

Jenna nodded, resolute, and reached up to kiss her son on the cheek.

"Don't let him go down the slide by himself," she said as she hurried to the sidewalk. "We don't want a repeat of him jumping off like last time!"

Riley waved her twin off and refocused on the tiny daredevil in question. Hartley was, thankfully, the spitting image of Jenna and not his father. A mop of red curls topped a matching pale complexion and smattering of freckles. The only differing trait was a set of bright green eyes. They followed Riley as she climbed up to the platform and settled down next to him. Together they hit the spinners and built-in music chimes.

Several minutes, and rides down the attached slide, went by without a text from Jenna. Riley hoped she could pull off her freelance career in Overlook, starting with Claire. As for her own career goals? Riley was still thinking about that. After her divorce many of her life plans had come to a screeching halt. She hadn't been able to rewrite them all yet.

"Hi!"

Hartley's high-pitched greeting flipped Riley's attention from setting herself up at the top of the slide again to someone standing a few feet from the stairs.

"Hi there."

The voice was deep, and for the briefest of moments, Riley hoped it belonged to Desmond Nash. Since he'd helped her, she'd had a hard time getting him out of her thoughts. It wasn't every day a cowboy businessman ran into the darkness to save you.

Yet, as her eyes traced the man's face, Riley didn't recognize him at all.

Stocky, on the shorter side and wearing business casual, his blue eyes swept over her and Hartley as he smiled.

Riley's instincts shot her hand out and looped her finger in the back of Hartley's shorts. She felt the strain as the always-curious toddler tried to toddle in the direction of the new person.

"Hi," Riley said from her spot sitting at the top of the jungle gym. Her legs were already on the slide but Hartley was still in roaming mode. The playground set they were on was meant for small children. It was only a three-or four-foot drop. It put her at the perfect height to have an even eye line with the man. It also made her instantly nervous with how close he was.

Riley knew not every smiling man was a Brett Calder, but that didn't stop the deep mistrust that had rooted within her.

It didn't help that the most precious human she knew was between them.

"I, uh, heard about what happened to your sister," he continued, taking a small step forward. "I was at the Second Wind party and we talked for a bit. It's crazy what happened to her, right?"

Red flags shot up all around Riley. He thought he was talking to Jenna. He was also lying.

She didn't remember talking to him at all.

"It was," she hedged, pulling Hartley closer. The park was a block from Main Street but there were several pedestrians walking across the sidewalk from the communal parking lot to the main strip. Plus, a few other parkgoers lounging around the benches and fountain in the center. Surely the man wouldn't do anything out in the open.

Calm down, Riley. This is a small town. He could be just a friendly townie. Maybe you did talk to him. You talked to so many people before you left!

The man was unaware of Riley's inner monologue. He pressed on.

"I actually work for the local newspaper and heard that maybe the more interesting story is you."

Riley couldn't help the eyebrow raise that followed that.

"You want to interview me?"

He shrugged.

"Why not? I heard you're a freelance designer—that's interesting. I heard you used to be part of a pretty successful company based in Kilwin—that's also interesting. I *also* heard you used to be married to the CFO before you left so fast one night you can probably still see the dust in the air."

The man grinned.

He was talking about Jenna.

Riley felt sick.

She didn't try to look inconspicuous as she moved backward and got to her feet. She pulled Hartley up with her.

"You've heard a lot," she said, voice swinging low into an angry thrum. Hartley started to squirm against her hip. Riley didn't let him down. "What did you say your name was?"

"I didn't."

He was still grinning.

Riley felt the weight of her cell phone in her back pocket. She was about to pull it out and call for help, potential misunderstandings be damned.

Maybe he saw she was on the verge of doing just that. He held up his hands in defense.

"Listen, I don't want any trouble. I just want to help get *your* side of the story out there, Ms. Stone. You know, what happened to your sister… And what happened between you and Ryan Alcaster."

If Riley could have spit fire, the man and the name he said with such nonchalance would have gone up in flames.

"Listen here," she started, instead. "You—"

"Geordi?" Another deep voice joined the area around them. This time it was someone other than Riley who whipped their head around at being addressed, and also, this time Riley recognized the newcomer.

Desmond was dressed down in a dark blue button up, a pair of jeans that looked like they were made just for him, a black Stetson and a pair of matching cowboy boots. Dark hair was flipping out beneath the rim on his hat and blue eyes that looked a whole lot more like the sky now that she could see them in the daytime were narrowed in on the man whose name was apparently Geordi. A blond-haired woman with a long braid over her shoulder, a scar on her left cheekbone and a sleeping baby in a sling across her chest stood next to Desmond. Her expression was impassive as she too was staring holes into the man.

"Well if it isn't the man of the hour," Geordi said with a notable lack of enthusiasm. He looked to the woman. "And the last Nash to get her week or two of fame."

"And if it isn't the ambulance-chasing has-been who took a perfectly good profession and decided to turn into a stereotypical scumbag instead. What brings you to town?"

Desmond said it with a smile but there was obviously no love there. Geordi looked ten shades of angry.

"Despite what you might believe, you don't own this town," he spit back. "Not only can I be here but I can talk to anyone I damn well want to."

"But does Ms. Stone want to talk to *you* is the question."

"I don't," Riley was quick to say. "In fact, I'd like to leave now."

Geordi let out a frustrated growl. Desmond didn't back down. He didn't break eye contact as he walked to the jungle gym's stairs and held out his hand. It was a power move if Riley ever did see one.

A power move that gave her the perfect way to get out of the reporter's vicinity.

She placed one hand inside the cowboy's and walked down the steps, careful to keep Hartley on her hip. He'd gone quiet, no doubt watching the growing group like a tennis enthusiast at Wimbledon.

"Then why don't you join us for coffee at Claire's? We were heading there just now."

Riley wasn't about to tell him that her sister *Jenna* was there in a meeting already. She also wasn't going to go to the car and leave Jenna either.

She definitely wasn't going to stay with Geordi.

"That sounds like a plan."

Desmond let go of her hand and, without prompting, went low and scooped up Jenna's "survival kit" for Hartley. It was a large messenger bag with a floral print across its length.

Desmond slung it over his shoulder like a man on a mission.

Then he tipped his hat to Geordi.

"You bother her again and I'll call the sheriff on you," he said, all cool. "If you really believe we Nashes run this town then imagine the trouble we could cause if we really wanted to."

DESMOND WAS SPITTING MAD.

Geordi Green was scourge of the earth, in his

humble opinion. A man who could barely be called a journalist let alone a decent human.

"Geordi runs an online tabloid out of his house near here," Madi explained when the three of them—five of them if you counted his niece, Addison, and the boy, one asleep the other watchful—were walking away from the man. "His plan of attack is to wait out the direct aftermath of when something big happens and then put a spin on it once everything has blown over. You know the 'calm before the storm'? Declan says Geordi is the 'crap after the storm.'"

"He's a pot stirrer," Desmond added.

"A big ol' crap pot stirrer," Madi finished.

Dark, worried eyes glanced back over their shoulder at the reporter. Desmond felt the need to defend her still pulsing through him. He slowed a beat and angled his body so he was between her and Geordi. Madi gave him a look but quickened her pace so they both were ahead of him.

Desmond realized the women hadn't met. He swallowed his bristling and remedied that.

"This is my sister Madi Mercer and my niece, Addison," he started. "Madi, this is Riley Stone."

Riley couldn't hide her look of surprise.

"You know I'm not Jenna?"

Desmond raised his eyebrow. Were they trying to switch *again*?

"Was I not supposed to?" Suspicion started to

rise in Desmond's chest again. He didn't understand the Stone twins if so.

Riley shook her head. She used her free hand
to point to Main Street a few yards away.

"No, I'm babysitting while Jenna is in a meeting with Claire." She actually laughed. "I'm honestly just surprised. I can't even count on one
hand how many people can tell us apart, not
even my—" The rest of the sentence died on her
tongue. A look of almost panic flashed across
her expression. She hurried to change whatever
she was about to say. "Most people just assume
whoever has Hartley is Jenna."

Desmond didn't see how. After he'd met the
real Jenna at the hospital, he'd noticed several
differences between them. The first and most noticeable being how she carried herself.

Jenna looked like she was always in a moment
of exhale, weighted and mentally sagging. The
entire world on her shoulders. When he found out
she was a single parent, Desmond assumed that's
where the worry must have been coming from.
He'd seen it on his own mother after their father
had passed away, even though the children had
all been grown.

Riley, on the other hand, held herself like she
was in a perpetual inhale. She stood taller and
at the ready. To the point of almost being de-
fensive. He'd seen that same stance clear as day
when talking to Geordi. She might have had her

nephew with her, but to Desmond, he'd known which sister she was with ease.

Although, if he had been unsure, the second she looked at him, he would have known.

Desmond knew it wasn't rational but after looking into the dark depths of Riley's eyes in the woods, he *knew* them.

It was a realization that made him uncomfortable.

Not only had she lied to him, even if it had been only for two hours, with everything going on Desmond didn't have the time to deal with anything other than Second Wind.

Especially not when people like Geordi Green were still circling.

Second Wind was about creating new beginnings for people who had survived being put through the wringer.

It was Desmond's greatest goal in life.

He didn't have room for anything else.

Not even a siren.

Chapter Seven

Geordi watched Desmond the Great and just another lamb who had fallen for his good-guy schtick walk away. The Nash daughter's presence wasn't surprising. The Nash clan had a habit of being together at almost all times. They did live together on the ranch like some weird commune.

Geordi didn't understand or appreciate the family's obsession with each other.

Just like he didn't understand his client's focus on the Stone twins.

He waited for Desmond and company to turn out of view before deciding to retreat to his car. There, he was and wasn't surprised to see a woman wearing an honest-to-God trench coat and sunglasses. How she thought that was being inconspicuous and her platinum-dyed and straight-as-a-board, down-to-her-hips hair wasn't an attention getter, he had no idea.

She lifted her designer frames and showed him something he assumed were smoky eyes. Geordi tried to keep up with what was "in," considering the only way to keep the tabloid alive was to be connected with the online world.

And, when that didn't work, take paying gigs like this one.

"That seemed to be a disaster," she greeted, eyes roaming to the sidewalk the group had just left. "You were supposed to talk to Jenna, not scare her into the arms of Mr. Dolittle."

Geordi felt his nostrils flare. Just as he felt the urge to strike out at the woman for talking to him like an errant child.

"It isn't my fault the Nash family moves across this town like a plague," he snarled out instead. "You can't throw a rock without hitting one of them and now that they're starting to reproduce? Forget about having peace and quiet in this town."

The woman didn't seem to understand the problem. She slid her sunglasses back up the bridge of her nose.

"I came to you looking for solutions, not problems," she simply stated. "If I had known you were so hung up on pretty boy and his famjam, I would have gone to someone else. A better reporter, for starters."

If it hadn't been midmorning on a Saturday near a park no less, Geordi would have given the woman a piece of his mind. A very loud piece.

"I can go to her house," he said through clenched teeth. It wasn't like finding it would be hard. There weren't many newcomers to Overlook. All he had to do was look at houses that had recently sold or been rented. Or just find Craig Tilly, the local Realtor, and buy him a drink.

The woman shook her head.

"The spotlight is already on the Stones. We don't want to get caught in it. Which is why it would have been so nice if you'd convinced her to come for an interview. I guess you lack charm and skills."

Geordi growled.

"Listen here, you little—"

The woman moved her coat. She pulled a small pistol out but didn't aim it at him. It was meant to be seen.

It was meant to threaten.

It did.

Geordi shut up.

The woman smiled but when she spoke her words were sharp.

"You made a promise. You agreed to a deal. But, more importantly, you took my money," she said. "Now it's up to you to figure out how to deliver what I've asked for. I don't care how you do it, just get it done or keeping that pathetic little blog up and running will be the least of your sleazy little worries. Understand?"

Every fiber of Geordi's being was telling him to walk away. To just leave. To maybe tell the woman off but from a safer distance.

But then he remembered all of that cash.

It would solve the entirety of his problems.

"Don't worry your pretty little head," he said. "I'll get her to talk to me."

"And when you do?"

"I'll make sure you're there for it."

The woman nodded, apparently satisfied. She turned on her heel but looked over her shoulder at him before she walked away.

"And, Mr. Green? You tell anyone about our little arrangement and I'll burn you and your life to the ground."

Geordi hated to admit it but he fully believed her.

SOMEHOW DESMOND'S MORNING had taken an unexpected turn.

He'd gone from giving in to his sister's request to put down his work and join her for coffee to sitting opposite a sea of red curls. Jenna and her son, Hartley, were in their own shared mom world with Madi and Addison while Claire moved between them to customers. It left Desmond and Riley sequestered to their non-children-filled lives at the end of the table.

Desmond took a long pull from his coffee. Riley picked at the sleeve on her cup. Those eyes, dark chocolate, met his after several minutes of pretending to be in the neighboring conversation before going right back into the fray.

It felt like she was avoiding him.

Desmond didn't like it.

"The coffee's good here, isn't it?"

If his brothers had been there they would have immediately gotten gruff with Desmond at his lame opener. The town of Overlook had dubbed him the charming Nash and here he was floundering about coffee.

Desmond blamed it on the sudden spike in anger he'd had at the sight of Geordi. His normal easygoing facade had taken a few hits recently and that sniveling pot stirrer had felt like a cherry on top.

He was off-balance and trying to reclaim his charisma.

But, Riley didn't make it easy.

The woman nodded, eyes meeting and settling in his gaze. They looked far away, lost in thought. A look he was used to seeing in the mirror. Then she took in a deep breath as if to shake herself out of it.

Maybe she hadn't been avoiding him after all.

"It is. Though, to be honest," Desmond's attention wobbled as she leaned in a little and lowered her voice, "I'm not a big coffee drinker—and yes, I know how insane that sounds—but that's how it's always been. Until now. I think there might be some kind of narcotic in here. I already want another cup and I'm not even halfway finished with this one."

Desmond chuckled.

"Welcome to Claire's," he said. "I grew up

on black coffee on the ranch but as soon as she opened her doors, she opened my eyes to these sugar monstrosities." He tapped his drink. "One second my eyes are drooping, the next I'm buzzing around, ready for anything."

"It's more of a hit or miss for me. I'm either energized and raring to go or I'm riding a sugar high all the way to a forced nap." Riley shrugged. "There's no pretty in-between for me."

Desmond saw the conversational bridge ahead unfurling. He knew what to say to get to the other side, just as he knew what to say to avoid it.

You just admitted to yourself you have no room for anything else in your life, his inner voice— angel or demon, he didn't rightly know which was speaking—goaded. *Smile, be nice, leave.*

Yet—

"Have you tried any of the other local eateries?" He thumbed back toward the wall behind him. "Like the Red Oak?"

"The Red Oak?" She shook her head. "I haven't been there."

Desmond felt a genuine smile split his face.

"Boy, you're missing out on that one. I spent the last few years traveling the country and *still* haven't found a restaurant that does it as good as the Oak. It's been around for almost my entire life. I swear it's one of the best things to come out of Overlook."

Leave it there, his inner voice warned.

But Desmond decided not to listen.

"I was actually going to go there tonight. Would you like to join me?"

One dinner wouldn't hurt anything, Desmond reasoned. It wouldn't *mean* anything. Just two friendly acquaintances sharing an old and new-found love for great food.

Right?

Then again, there was something about Riley Stone. Something that made him feel different.

Maybe it wasn't a good idea after all.

No sooner had Desmond's reasoning slipped by, than it was replaced by a startling smile in answer.

"That sounds nice. Sure."

Reasoning or not, Riley was ten kinds of beautiful, a fact he couldn't much deny anymore.

And she was smiling right at him.

"IS THIS A DATE?"

That question had punctuated the second half of Desmond's Saturday with annoying precision. Madi, who did *not* live on the ranch anymore, had come back to the Nash family ranch with stubborn persistence and there she had stayed, up until Desmond was getting into his truck.

"*Is* this a date?" she started, hurrying alongside him. Their mother stood on the porch—another woman who had copied the question and thrown it at Desmond at every chance she had gotten—holding Addison while Julian had agreed to man their bed-and-breakfast so Madi could keep up her verbal assaults. Apparently Desmond was known for being charming but not known for using that charm to go on dates. Not that he was counting dinner with Riley as a date, he'd decided. It was just two people who had been tangled up in each other's lives recently sharing a friendly meal. That was it. "Because *if it is*, I just want to remind you of a few things before you go."

Desmond sighed. If he wasn't so annoyed, he would have taken pleasure in seeing his breath mist out in front of him. February had a habit of unpredictable weather. They'd gone from warm to humid to chill to now, a high chance of rain and a low of thirty-eight. He'd had to break out his leather jacket. It was thick, insulated and had once belonged to his father.

He burrowed his hands into the worn pockets and waited for his sister to catch up. He leaned against the truck door and looked at her expectantly as she started grinning across from him.

"It's not a date," he reminded her. "But say what you want to so you, Ma and the little one don't freeze on my account."

Madi dropped her grin. She got down to business.

. "I was going to say *if this is* a date, try not to look like that." She put her thumb between his eyebrows. It was ice-cold. He swatted her away, startled.

"Like what, Crazy Lady?"

"Like you're not there," she stressed. "Be *present*. Leave work on the way, way, way back burner and don't worry about the construction site or reporters, Geordi Green included." She grabbed the opening of his jacket and pulled the sides closer together, a maternal move that softened his annoyance with her. "You can help people live their lives while still living your own. Have *fun*. Even if this isn't a date, that doesn't mean you can't enjoy it. Got it, cowboy?"

Desmond snorted.

"I got it, cowgirl. Thanks."

Madi nodded, satisfied. She let him get into the truck before she issued one last comment.

"And Des? Ma and I have decided to not tell those other two Nashes about this nondate until tomorrow." She smirked. "Enjoy the freedom."

Desmond didn't say so but he did appreciate that gesture.

Winding Road led him to the county road that took him across town to one of the more rural Overlook neighborhoods called Willows Way. Ranch-style houses were planted on large lots with at least a half acre or so between each. While there were an insane amount of trees taking over most of the town, Willows Way had very few. Some of the residents had compensated by creating massive gardens, statue scenes and one even had soccer goals planted in the yard.

Desmond hadn't been to Willows Way in years. In fact, he hadn't been to the opposite side of Overlook at all in some time. Actually, he hadn't been on a social call in general in a while either.

It made him weirdly antsy.

Was he nervous?

Why should he be?

Desmond swore as he cut the engine in the driveway of the all brick house at 207 Willows Way.

"Madi got to me," he told no one.

The home was smaller than the other houses on the road but there was a charm to it. Yet when movement from inside caught his eye, a surge of adrenaline rocketed through him. Desmond's muscles tensed, a dull ache in his leg throbbed and he was seconds away from jumping out of the truck and running inside to rescue anyone who needed it.

But then he felt like an idiot. It took him a few beats of being completely still to realize he had overreacted. The movement belonged to a woman peering out the window then moving and making the curtains sway.

Maybe he was a little more on edge about this nondate—and in general—than he'd admitted.

Desmond took one long breath and told his body to calm down.

Sometimes life could be simple.

There was no reason to believe anything else was going to get messy.

When his cell phone started to ring, Desmond decided he'd listen to Madi's advice. He'd ignore the call. Enjoy his dinner and company. He'd *be present*. He could call whoever it was back. No problem.

But curiosity was a persistent creature. Once he saw the caller ID Desmond couldn't help but click Accept.

Why was one of the town lawyers calling him?

He answered the phone with one hand on the door handle.

"Desmond, here."

"Hey, Desmond, it's Marty McLinnon."

"Hey, Marty, what can I do you for?"

There was rustling on the other side of the phone. Marty was moving around.

"Well, I was at home when I got an alert that the cameras at my law office across the street from your construction site were going off. Since what happened the other week I pointed one of my cameras in that direction and *that's* the one that picked up something. I looked into the live feed and there sure was some movement so I drove on out here and parked in the back and—" There was movement again. The man was breathing a bit harder than normal. "Yep, there's someone in the building. I can see them on the second floor. You got anyone that's supposed to be up there?"

Desmond shook his head even though the man couldn't see him. His adrenaline spiked again. This time with a vengeance.

"Not on a Saturday night, no."

"That's what I thought." Marty started to lower his voice. "Hey, Desmond, my husband is calling. Probably freaking out. I need to get it. Want me to call the cops after?"

"I'll call Declan—don't worry. Just don't go over there, okay? Could be some punk teens being rebellious, could be worse."

"I got you. I'll stay put."

"Thanks, Marty."

The call ended. Desmond got out of the truck, phone to his ear and called Declan on reflex.

"Marty McLinnon is across from Second Wind right now. He says there's someone on the second floor," he jumped in.

Declan was quick to answer. Though there was some heat in his voice.

"Call Caleb. I'm—I'm in a situation right now. Call me if anything else happens."

The phone call ended without another word.

Desmond did as he was told.

Caleb didn't answer, which was unusual. When Jazz's phone went straight to voice mail, the hair on the back of Desmond's neck rose. Something must have been going on with the department. Something pressing.

He hoped his family was okay.

In the meantime, Desmond decided not to call anyone else.

Not until he was on-site. The drive wasn't too far from where he was now. He could join Marty and try to take a picture of the culprit, if he or she *was* a culprit. Plus, if Marty's camera caught the person already, they could use that to ID them if they were gone by the time he showed up. Plus, the department wasn't too far away from Second Wind's construction site anyways.

Desmond was about to run up to the Stone sisters' door and cancel their plans when the front door opened.

He found those dark eyes, framed by crimson fire, and knew then, with surprising ferocity, that he didn't want to cancel at all. Not on Riley.

Not even when his gut was twisting to get a move on and protect his baby, Second Wind.

No. Desmond knew right at that moment that he didn't want to leave without her.

Chapter Eight

What Desmond Nash would never know was just how insane the Stone household became leading up to the moment he arrived at the front door.

"He's here," Jenna had yelled clear across the house. She'd had her nose basically pressed against the living-room window for twenty minutes in anticipation of the man's arrival. Riley had been taken aback by Desmond's casual invite to dinner; Jenna had lost her damn mind.

"Have you seen him?" Jenna had exclaimed when they'd gotten in the car after Claire's. "He's not even my type and my knees went a bit gooey when he *shook my hand*. I mean I saw him at the hospital the other day, sure, but without the adrenaline and sisterly worry I really got to see him, you know? He's like *a cowboy* and he loves his family... I mean, wow-ee!"

Riley wasn't going to disagree.

"So, let me be the first to say, I totally get why you said yes," Jenna had continued. "But, I *do* have to ask, is it a date?"

That had been a question that both women had gone over the rest of the day. Riley didn't think it was, Jenna wanted it to be. The uncertainty ate at Jenna until it had manifested in Riley mere minutes before he was supposed to arrive.

After Jenna had heralded his arrival, chaos had consumed the house.

"What's he wearing?" Riley had yelled back. Jenna's bed was covered in ten different outfits all of varying levels of heat. From completely casual jeans and a button up to a little black dress with heels that tied up and across the ankle.

Jenna had gone silent.

"JENNA?"

"He's still in the truck! I can't see what he's wearing!"

Riley had felt like an idiot as she waited. Mostly because she was standing in her black bra-and-panty set staring at a pile of clothes.

"He's getting out," Jenna had finally yelled.

Riley's muscles had tensed up. Her adrenaline had hit a high. She had waited with bated breath until…

"Dressy casual! Outfit number three!" Footsteps had thundered down the hallway as Jenna flew into the room. She had panted while she repeated herself. "Dressy. Casual."

Riley had dressed faster than she ever had in her entire life. Outfit number three was a Stone sister combo. Jenna's black skinny jeans and suede boots, Riley's navy sheer blouse and faux leather bomber jacket.

"Date or no date, you look hot! Now, teeth."

Jenna had performed the lipstick check before running behind Riley and fluffing her hair. It was down and crazy, as per usual.

Now after opening the front door because Riley couldn't take it anymore, Jenna crouched down behind the oak door, out of sight. She looked like a crazy person.

"Have fun and wear protection," she hissed.

Riley's cheeks turned into flames.

There was a special kind of chaos that came with being a sister.

"Hey there," Riley greeted, lamely. She already felt off her game around Desmond but Jenna had really thrown her off, especially since Riley knew she was behind the door, listening. It pushed her to almost jump across the door frame, closing that same door shut as she did so.

Desmond watched the move but didn't offer a comment.

Or the greeting Riley had expected.

"Do you mind if we make a quick pit stop?"

Riley, still very much wanting to create distance between them and her eavesdropping sister, was already walking toward him.

"That sounds fine to me!"

Desmond was stepping fast. He paused only

long enough to open the door for her. He was in his seat in record time.

"Is something wrong?" she couldn't help but ask. The urgency was clear, she just didn't know what for.

Desmond, who was absolutely owning a dark red button-down, dark jeans and a worn leather jacket that actually matched hers, made a noise in response.

A weird noise.

One that had her turning in her seat with her eyebrow rising high. She saw Desmond glance at her out of his periphery. He turned the engine over. His hand went to the gear shift but he stopped from putting it in Reverse.

He sighed.

Then there were baby blues staring at her.

"I just got a call that someone is lurking around Second Wind's construction site. I think it might be the person who vandalized a wall there the night of the gala. The department seems to have their hands full so I thought I'd go check it out before I call in the rest of cavalry. We can reschedule if you want. It's really no problem."

Riley slapped her seat belt into the clasp with vigor.

"Come on! Let's go before he gets away!"

Desmond's eyes widened in surprise but he got to reversing without making any more fuss.

"I didn't know the construction site was vandalized before," she admitted. It was a bizarre desire to want to be a part of seeing if someone was messing with Second Wind but there Riley was, feeling it.

"Yeah, it was one of the few pieces of news the media around here didn't find and publish. Honestly, I'm okay with that."

"Wait, is that the reason you were on Winding Road when Brett—well, when *that* happened?"

He nodded.

"I slipped away to check it out for myself after my brothers told me. Second Wind, it—it means a lot to me so I wanted to see it in person. I saw the wreck on my way back to the party."

"I'm sorry it happened, the vandalism, but I have to say I'm extremely lucky it did." Riley lightened her tone. "Maybe count the first strike as a necessary evil so you could convert another person to your obsession with this Red Oak place? Is that an okay silver lining?"

A small smile tugged up on the corner of Desmond's lips.

"I suppose so because it really *is* a great place. Their steak?" He brought the tips of his fingers to his mouth and kissed them dramatically. "*Perfecto.* Unless…" A look of acute worry immediately blanketed his expression.

Riley realized, belatedly, she was just staring at the man like he was a riveting action movie playing on a TV.

He didn't seem to care when he whipped his head around to look her in the eye.

"Unless you're vegan? Or a vegetarian?"

Riley laughed.

"Neither."

Desmond let out an exhale of relief.

"I mean, they have salads and other options but the steak and chicken? As Madi says sometimes when something is really good, 'God bless.'"

The urgency, the tension the cowboy had been carrying seemed to lessen. Riley wanted to capitalize on that. She turned her gaze out the windshield, watching the dark world around them flash by. In the woods it had been terrifying. Here, with Desmond in the truck, it was actually comforting.

"I know everyone assumes multiples *have* to be close but it's nice to see you seem to genuinely be close with your siblings," she said. "I also have to admit, I've never met a set of triplets before. It's kind of exciting."

Desmond let out a howl of laughter. Riley jumped in surprise. It only seemed to balloon that same laughter.

"The other day Caleb and I talked about how wild it was to meet a set of identical twins." He turned, pulling her attention from the road outside. "Like I told him, it's like looking in a mirror with the two of you. What was that like growing up? We're fraternal and Madi still felt like she had to dye her hair blond to feel like an individual."

It was a question Riley and Jenna had been asked a lot growing up. One, she suspected, she'd always get asked. It was also the most she thought Desmond had spoken to her in one breath.

"We went through a phase where we tried to look different. Coincidentally it was the same time I realized that, yes, mohawks are a daring hairstyle but not everyone was meant to rock them." Desmond snorted. They turned out of the neighborhood and bounced along an even darker road. "Other than that I can't say we've ever really disliked being identical twins. Then again, I think I got incredibly lucky with who ended up being mine." A warmth blossomed in Riley's chest. It was followed by a low flame of anger. Old but always hot. She knew she sounded different when she continued. "Jenna is one of those people who has the rare capability to love unconditionally *even* when it's not deserved. She's good people through and through. I think that's what's made being her twin so easy. I don't just like being her sister, I'm proud to be."

The sudden rush of enthusiasm on Desmond's part diminished. Riley felt her cheeks heat. She'd overshared.

"Feel free not to answer but that love that's not deserved, does it have to do with Hartley's father?"

Yep. She'd overshared.

Still, she answered. Though she did so carefully.

"Yes. At first he seemed like the perfect guy. But then… He wasn't." Riley couldn't help her hand from fisting in her lap. Guilt, heavy and hollowing pushed through the fire in her chest. "She stayed with him longer than she should have, so worried leaving would hurt Hartley. Worried that somehow it was her fault too. It took a lot for her to realize that the only good option was to go." She unfurled her fist and took a small breath. "Then she came here, fell in love with the town and rented the first house she saw. At first I think it was a temporary plan but now I think she's in for the long haul."

"Overlook can have that effect on people. How do you like it? Declan said you said you lived in Atlanta before coming here? That's definitely a far cry from small-town Tennessee."

She nodded.

"It is," she admitted. "But it's not bad. Just different. I used to work as an office manager for a company that was in the heart of downtown. The commute was…less than desirable. I don't miss that."

"But you do miss it? The city, I mean."

Riley had thought about that a lot since she'd arrived with all of her belongings on Jenna's doorstep.

"I miss the rhythm. The hustle and bustle. Even though there were so many people doing so many things, I grew used to it. Here, well, I don't think I've really left the house enough to learn the rhythm."

She caught the small smile tugging at the corner of his lips again.

"You ever had a faucet with a slow leak?" he asked. "One that just goes *drip…drip…drip…* I'd say that's about our speed in good ol' Overlook."

Riley wanted to point out that in the short time she'd been there she'd been chased by a man into the woods with a bat and then approached by a scoundrel reporter who had done such a good job at digging, he'd hit the one deep wound she and her sister shared. Instead she laughed.

"A leak is better than a flood, I suppose."

A small silence stretched between them. Riley didn't know how to fill it. But she knew she wanted to do just that. She wanted to learn more about the man next to her.

Sure, Desmond Nash was a good-looking guy. He was the poster boy for strapping young cowboys who could use their jawlines to slice butter. Yet, there was more to the man than looks. Tragedy had shaped him as far as Riley could surmise from the countless news stories. He'd taken that pain and made it into a tool. One that had created a foundation that was now setting up shop in the same town he'd experienced that tragedy.

There was a weight to Desmond.

Riley couldn't explain it past that. She'd felt it looking into his eyes that night in the woods, she'd felt it seeing his anger at her lie in the hospital and she'd felt it now sitting next to him.

Desmond Nash was a question she wanted to answer and an answer she wanted to question. All at once.

SECOND WIND'S CONSTRUCTION SITE was five minutes from downtown Overlook. Placed on a large lot bordered by pines, it was one of five businesses along the aptly named Business Boulevard. A back road led to the law offices across the street and the florist farther down. Desmond took it slow and with the truck's lights off until they were parked next to Marty McLinnon's Honda at the law offices.

"I don't think anyone is in there," Riley said, face an inch from the passenger's-side window. She unbuckled her seat belt without looking. "Do you think this Marty guy is inside of the offices?"

Desmond undid his own seat belt. A trickle of excitement ran down his spine, spiked by the excitement he heard in her voice.

"Let's find out."

They moved from the truck to the back door of the office building. It was locked. Desmond knocked but no response. He pulled out his phone and called Marty back.

After a moment Riley touched his arm. She turned her head toward the corner of the building.

"Do you hear that?"

Desmond lowered the phone. It took him a moment to hear a song playing somewhere out in the night. It was faint.

"It sounds so far away," Riley whispered. They followed the length of the building to the corner. Like they were in an episode of *Scooby-Doo*, they leaned over and peeked around the brick. It gave them a clear view of the other side of the road.

To Second Wind.

To where the ringing was coming from.

Right before it stopped.

Marty's voice mail started to play.

"Call back to make sure that's his phone we're hearing." The excitement Desmond had heard in Riley's voice earlier was ebbing. "You told him not to go over there, right?"

Desmond called the number again.

"Yeah, but Marty's stubborn as nails. It's what makes him a good lawyer." The call went through. The music started playing in the distance again. "Me telling him to not go over there might have just convinced him to do the opposite."

"Would he confront whoever it was lurking?"

"Same answer."

Riley turned around. It made him realize how close they were. The smell of lavender filled his senses.

"What do you want to do?"

Dark, entrancing, mesmerizing.

Riley Stone didn't realize the power she could conjure with just one even stare.

It inspired a cocktail of emotions within him. The most potent? Bravado.

"I'm going to go see who's been messing with my site."

A faint smile tugged at Riley's lips. She nodded.

"After you."

Desmond opened his mouth to complain; Riley held up her hand. It was mere inches from his chest.

"I'm going with you. Here." She opened the purse she'd been wearing across her chest. What she pulled out made Desmond chuckle. He saw his breath mist out in front of him.

"Pepper spray?"

"You bet your boots, cowboy. Now let's get going."

Desmond tipped his hat.

"Yes, ma'am."

Business Boulevard was lit by tall and relatively new streetlamps that stood every hundred yards or so. The construction site had four separate lights that bathed each corner in enough light meant to dissuade any theft or vandalism.

A lot of good that had done.

Desmond led the way from the streetlamp's

circle of illumination and past a parked Bobcat at the front of the site.

"If anyone is on the second or third floors, I can't see them," Riley whispered at his side. She was so close again her hair was brushing against his arm and back.

Distracting.

But not as much as the unease growing in his stomach.

Second Wind was mostly just a skeleton of beams and partially constructed walls. There were tarps and stacks of building materials and slight mayhem everywhere. A set of stairs that had been constructed but weren't finished. It still got workers to the upper two floors. The start of the steps was housed in the section of the first floor that was tucked out of sight from the front of the building.

In front of them now, on an expanse of constructed exterior wall, was where the graffiti had been before.

Can't even win a simple game of hide-and-seek.

Those words had been painted over, the only part of the wall that was light gray.

There was no movement near it or them.

Without a word Desmond called Marty again.

This time it went straight to voice mail.

Desmond and Riley shared a look.

His gut started yelling.

He should have listened.

Instead they wordlessly went through the opening and into the first floor. Riley pulled out her phone and switched it to flashlight mode. The new light made shadows skitter over the concrete.

"Empty."

They fanned out across the expanse. Desmond shook his head.

Where was Marty?

Where was the person he'd seen?

Was this some kind of tasteless prank?

Another jab at Desmond to create a new surge of press?

"Desmond?"

He turned around, pulling up his call log as he did so, ready to call the sheriff's department, but paused when he saw Riley's expression.

Wide eyes. Wide, worried eyes. She was pointing to the stairs in the corner.

"Is that…?"

Desmond looked to where she was pointing. No one was there but something was on the ground. With soft steps he made his way over, his gut yelling even louder.

Riley's light ran across the blood just as Desmond realized what it was.

"Call 9-1-1."

Riley didn't listen. Instead she angled her phone up the dark tunnel that ran up the stairs.

"It leads up there," she whispered. "Marty might be hurt."

Desmond caught her hand, the one holding the pepper spray.

It wasn't enough to calm his fraying nerves.

"We don't know—"

Something large dropped from the second floor to the dirt across from them, just outside of the first-floor concrete. Riley yelled out in surprise. He tightened his grip around her hand.

The something grunted.

Desmond couldn't believe his eyes.

That something was a man.

And it wasn't Marty McLinnon.

Chapter Nine

Desmond took off running. Riley would have been on his heels but she heard something he didn't.

It was a shuffling sound.

And it was coming from the top of the stairs.

Desmond and the man, who she was assuming wasn't his buddy Marty, had kicked up dust and were booking it toward the road. Riley wasn't about to yell for him to come back. She wasn't about to wait for him either.

She ran a thumb under the strap of her purse across her chest to the main part of the bag, securing it while tightening her grip around the pepper spray. The light from her cell phone in the other hand made the blood look glossy.

Riley was careful not to step on it as she took the stairs up two at a time.

The second floor had three walls. Where the fourth was going to be was open and showed the law offices across the street. The closest streetlamp did a better job of illuminating this floor than the one below it.

Along with the man standing in the middle of the space.

Riley was stunned with how well dressed he was. So well dressed, in fact, that it was the first detail she registered. A dark gray suit, three-piece, and shoes that absolutely shone. His hair was dirty blond and combed against his scalp. He had his hands in his pockets like he was waiting for a client to arrive. He even looked at Riley like she was the one who'd come in for the meeting with him.

One that she had been late for.

His tone bit like he was chiding her, yet his words were nothing but alarming.

"Marty McLinnon, husband to one and father to four, is on the third floor of this construction site and battling for his life." He nodded toward the wall to her left. "If there was a window right there you'd see a section of a support beam attached to a chain. That beam is getting lower and lower because it's either dragging an unconscious Mr. McLinnon to the edge of the building or slowly pulling his legs out of joint. I'm not sure which is happening but I'm pretty sure if you don't get up there right now and start cutting through that chain he's going to be in a bad way."

Riley waited for the man to laugh, to say *just kidding*, and then say, "Hey! I'm Marty McLinnon. Did you see that crazy man jump to the ground floor?"

But he didn't.

Instead he bent down, picked something up off the floor and held it out to her.

It was a power tool.

No.

It was a handheld electric saw. Riley knew because she'd seen her dad use a similar one to do drywall work at their home in Georgia.

"You'll need to plug it in but this should cut through the chain," he added. "Drop the pepper spray and your phone and I'll give it to you. If not, I'll throw it off the building and we can hear it break. Just like we'll hear Mr. McLinnon break if you don't decide soon."

He shook the saw.

Riley didn't know the man. *Nothing* about him was familiar. The light and shadows were playing tricks on her eyes. One second he looked younger than her, in the next he had the nonchalance of a wiser, much older man.

However, what she *was* sure of?

This wasn't a joke to him.

Riley dropped her phone and pepper spray. Their *thud*s against the concrete echoed around the unfinished space.

"Who are you?" she had to ask.

The man shook his head. Then he nodded to the stairs.

"That blood had to come from someone and it didn't come from me. The longer you're on this floor, the shorter Mr. McLinnon's life span becomes."

Riley felt like she was having an out-of-body experience. Yet, she ran over to him and took the saw, careful to grab the cord off of the ground.

"Ticktock, Ms. Stone."

DESMOND'S LEG WAS HURTING but the man he was chasing also seemed to be favoring one leg over the other. The jump from the second story had no doubt been less than pleasant.

"Stop," Desmond yelled again.

The man didn't.

They streaked past Business Boulevard in the direction of the law office's parking lot. The man in black had enough of a lead that, when he tripped over the curb, he was able to get back up and start running again. Though he had slowed considerably.

"Stop, dammit!"

Again, the man didn't listen.

He turned so he was running along the back road. That surprised Desmond. If he had been trying to lose someone, he would go into the trees. Yet the man stayed on the road.

It made up Desmond's mind.

He spun around and pulled out his car keys. Hurrying back to his truck, he threw himself inside the cab and turned the engine.

He couldn't follow the man into the trees but

if he stayed on the road that was something Desmond could work with.

The tires squealed as the truck reversed. Before popping the gear into Drive he hit Declan's number on his recent-calls list and put it on speaker. It started ringing. Desmond pressed down the gas.

"Des, can I call—"

"We found blood at the construction site and then a man dressed in all black jumped from the second story and took off," Desmond jumped in. "I'm chasing him now in my truck because he's sticking to the back road."

The man glanced over his shoulder. His eyes widened in the headlights' beam. He angled off the road and into the grass. Still he didn't run into the trees.

"Does he have a weapon?" Declan had become completely focused. His tone was curt.

"Not that I can tell. But we haven't seen Marty anywhere and, Dec, I never called in the troops."

Declan swore.

"Hold on," he said in the next breath. He started talking to someone.

Desmond was coming up on the man in black. He was continuing to slow down.

"I'm about to get this guy," he told his older brother.

The truck took to the grass and dirt and the small slope down like a champ. Desmond sped up and turned the wheel, kicking up dirt as he went, and then hit the brakes hard.

The man in black stopped just as abruptly and turned. Desmond realized then that the man had every intention of finally running to the trees, a place he didn't have the clearance to drive his truck between, but then he tripped again.

This time he didn't get back up.

Desmond was out of the truck in a flash.

The man pulled himself up into a sitting position. His head was bent over. He was panting.

Desmond had a lot of questions.

He started with the most pressing.

"Where's Marty McLinnon?"

The man didn't get a chance to react.

They both turned as a scream echoed out across the night air.

It was Riley.

And she was yelling for him.

THE CHAIN TORE at her hands.

"No!"

Riley pulled with all her might. She was standing between the unobstructed edge of the third floor and the limp body of a man who was sliding to his potential death. The motion had been slow when she'd first gotten to his side, but as she'd looked around for an outlet, he'd made a noise.

That noise had heralded a truly terrifying sight. One that made her drop the saw and run. Marty's body had hit something slick covering that section of the floor. Whether it was blood, oil or water, Riley didn't have the time to find out.

It had sped up his movement, whatever it was.

Now Riley was trying and failing to pull the section of support beam up. A foolish attempt. She barely got her hands beneath the chain to pull in the first place.

Something hit the back of her foot.

It was Marty's boot.

Riley let out a strangled gasp, surprised he'd already made it to where she was.

A ball of ice exploded in her gut, filling her veins.

There wasn't enough room between them and the edge. Riley couldn't pull the beam up. She didn't have enough time to find an outlet and cut it. Not with how fast he was sliding now.

She'd already called for Desmond but he wasn't there.

Was she about to watch this poor man go over the edge?

"No no no no no."

Riley abandoned the chain and spun around to focus on a Hail Mary plan. It took a few seconds and was in no way a good idea but Riley didn't care.

She unbuckled her belt and flung it off in two seconds flat. Moving catty-cornered to a steel beam already erected, she threw the belt around the metal and buckled it back. Marty's body kept sliding. She let him until his arm was level with her.

Riley sat her butt down and put a death grip on her belt. Then she grabbed Marty McLinnon's arm.

The tension came shortly after. Riley's stomach nearly turned as she felt the weight trying its best to pull Marty away. If he had been awake, she had no doubt the pain would have been awful.

"Come on, come on," she chanted, having no idea who she was chanting to.

That's when she heard the vehicle approaching. Tires skidded to a stop somewhere near the front of the building. Then Riley heard a sound that temporarily pushed the cold from her veins.

"Riley?"

It was Desmond.

"Up here," she yelled. "Third floor! *Hurry!*"

The pull from the beam was getting worse. Riley tried to stay where she was but the pull was too strong. She was starting to slide herself.

"No!"

Marty's arm lifted above his head and she had to move her grip to his wrist. Her nails bit painfully into the palm of her hand as her hold on the belt tightened with the strain.

Footsteps thundered up the stairs. Riley knew there wasn't time to explain everything. She craned her neck around to see the bewildered expression of the most handsome man she'd ever known and hoped he knew how to handle an electric saw.

"Find an outlet," she yelled in greeting. She could hear the pain in her voice as it started to feel like she was being pulled apart. She couldn't imagine how Marty felt. "There's the saw!"

Desmond, bless him, was quick on the uptake.

He grabbed the saw off of the ground and ran purposefully toward them, stopping to plug it in.

A horrible, twisting worry occurred to Riley then.

What if the cord wasn't long enough to reach the chain?

"It'll reach," Desmond said, answering her thought without realizing it. He slid across the space between it and the chain. Riley squeezed her eyes shut but didn't quell her cry of pain.

A small part of her had hoped the chain was long enough that the beam would hit the ground soon and stop the pull. Yet, it just wasn't happening.

The sound of the saw was a beautiful one. The noise of it eating through the chain was magical.

However, it was a slow process.

By the time he'd cut through the top part of the link, Riley was struggling. Blood was coming out of the hand holding the belt just as blood was coming out of Marty's hand as her grip was maxed out on him.

She felt like a rubber band about to break; her entire body was angled toward the edge.

If she let go, Marty would only have a foot before he was falling through the air.

"Hurry," she yelled. "I can't hold on much longer!"

Desmond didn't respond. It wasn't like he could say anything to help.

Riley squeezed her eyes shut again. A few more seconds passed until, in the darkness behind her lids, she realized another horrifying thought.

The beam was too heavy.

She was about to let go.

"I can't—"

Before she could finish her sentence, Marty McLinnon's hand slid out of hers.

Riley's eyes flashed open, horrified she was about to watch a man fall to his death.

What she saw instead was Desmond as he let out a body-sagging exhale, a severed chain between them.

Marty had finally stopped moving.

Two baby blues found their way to her. He had questions, which was okay because she had answers. But when he dropped the saw and hurried over to her, all Riley could do was express the immense relief she was feeling.

"I'm so sorry I left—" Desmond started, but the moment he was within arm's reach, Riley pulled him down to her.

He hit his knees with a grunt. She fully realized it probably hurt but then she pushed herself up and against him and did exactly what she thought needed to be done.

Their lips crashed together with a smack that echoed. Riley threw her arms around the man's neck like he was a lifeline and she was on the brink.

The kiss was hard but it unfurled something inside her that she hadn't realized had been there in the first place. Her unexpected weight against him sent them backward to the concrete she'd now despise forever. Her arms around his neck kept his head from connecting with that same floor.

Riley ended the kiss as quickly as she had initiated it.

Then she was lying on top of the man and staring into his eyes.

"Thank you," she said, breathless.

Thank you for not letting a man die because I couldn't hold on.

Thank you for not questioning me when I needed you to do something.

Thank you for coming back.

Riley dropped her head against his chest, realizing how tired she was. For the second time since she'd met the man, he held her in silence for a much-needed second or two.

Then she remembered why she was there in the first place.

"There was a man in a suit here," she hurried, rolling off him without an ounce of grace. "He gave me the saw when I dropped my phone and spray. He told me Marty was about to die."

Desmond's brow knitted together. He pulled his phone from his pocket. He had Declan on speaker phone.

"We're almost there," the sheriff yelled out. "EMT should be right on our tails."

Desmond reached over to check Marty's pulse. He nodded to Riley.

"Marty is alive," he yelled to the phone. "I'm— *We're* going to go get the other man to make sure he doesn't escape."

Desmond pulled Riley to her feet and kept hold of her hand. Wordlessly they got into his truck near the open first floor of the construction site and then drove across the street. Riley was about to ask where they were going as they headed toward the back road they'd come in on when she saw a figure on the side of the road.

"I hog-tied him with some rope I had from the barn," he explained when they stopped. The headlights showed the man in all black lying on his stomach on the grass, his arms, wrists and ankles tied up behind him. "I wasn't sure it would hold since I did it so quick."

He started to get out as the man ahead of them turned toward the truck.

Riley sucked in a breath.

Desmond stalled next to his opened door.

"What is it?" he asked, voice already drowning in concern.

Riley didn't speak for a moment.

There's no way...

"Riley?"

A warm hand touched hers. Another grabbed her chin. Desmond gently turned her head.

Riley looked into those crystal blue eyes, so blue she felt like she could swim in them, and said something she never thought she'd utter in Overlook.

"That's my ex-husband."

Chapter Ten

Hitting something seemed too dramatic. The walls of Declan's office in Wildman County's sheriff's department hadn't done anything to Desmond. It seemed unfair to take out his anger and frustration there.

Yelling also didn't seem the best course of action.

Declan and the uniforms who had shown up at the construction site now knew as much as he did. Cussing at them didn't get anyone anywhere. Plus, it was rude.

And not what the most charming Nash was expected to do.

What everyone probably expected of him was to be a cool cucumber. Ready to go with an easy smile and a tip of the hat.

But that wasn't him.

Not right now.

Riley was sitting next to him in an old wing-back chair that made her seem impossibly small. She had bandages across each of her palms and they were resting on the tops of her thighs. When she caught him staring, her smile was weak.

Since the revelation that the man in black was her ex-husband, they hadn't gotten a chance to be alone together. Definitely not talk in private. Now, after Declan had told them to wait in his office, was the perfect time to tackle whatever the hell was going on together.

Yet for all Desmond's fame of being the smooth one of the Nash bunch, he was finding that with Riley his words often were raw. He didn't have a prepared speech or thought to share.

He was at a loss and it manifested in nearly palpable hesitation.

One that Riley broke, despite Desmond's intentions to do it first.

"Can we rain check dinner at the Red Oak?"

Desmond offered a weak smile in return.

"I'd be okay with that."

Riley nodded.

"Good. Good."

Silence pushed between them again.

Desmond glanced down at her lips. The same ones that had crushed his at the construction site.

It wasn't the time, the place or the situation to be thinking about them. Yet, there he was. Wishing he could have a do-over. He hadn't kissed back because, honestly, he'd been too surprised.

Now he wasn't.

Now he wanted to.

Now wasn't the time.

The door opened and Declan walked in. His hat had been off since they'd arrived at the department. That usually meant business.

"Marty's husband and kids are at the hospital with Detective Santiago," he said, going to his chair and taking a seat. "He's hurt, but unless something changes, he'll be fine. Eventually. Before you arrived it appears he was knocked out pretty hard. There's a nasty cut on his scalp, explaining all that blood."

"What about his legs?" Riley asked.

Declan looked unsure of what to say. Desmond spoke up.

"Better off than if he'd fallen unconscious three stories, I can tell you that."

Riley gave him a look riddled with guilt. He wanted to wipe it away.

"I know Marty," he added. "Whatever injuries he takes from this he'll gladly accept over the alternative. You saved his life."

Declan nodded his agreement.

Riley visibly let a long breath out.

Then it was back to business.

"As for the man in the suit, we have a BOLO out on him based on your description. Caleb is also at the law offices looking at their security footage with one of the other partners." It was Declan's turn to let out a sigh. "Which brings us to the one man out of the three who can tell us what in the heck was going on out there."

Riley stiffened. Desmond, in response, did too.

"Davies," she said, anger threading clear through the two syllables.

Her ex-husband.

Desmond felt the heat of jealousy push against his gut. He tried to remember that it was her ex, but still, the thought of another man with her put fire in him.

Not the time, he scolded himself, again.

"That's his last name, right?" Declan asked.

She nodded.

"He hates the name Evan so everyone calls him by his last name. It was the reason why I didn't take his name when we married. He said it felt like I was stealing a part of his identity."

Desmond snorted.

He'd be proud as hell for Riley to wear his name if she wanted it.

Declan shot him a look and stood up.

"I don't normally do this but Marty is a well-established member of Overlook and, well, we're coming up with a lot more questions than I'm comfortable with," he said. "I'd appreciate if you could come observe the interrogation. You know this Davies better than any of us so you might be able to pick up on something we won't be able to."

Riley stood. Hesitation lined her body.

"He won't be able to see me, right?"

"Right. You'll be behind a two-way mirror. We won't even let him know you're in the building." Declan opened the door and waved a deputy over. "Can you take Ms. Stone to the viewing room? We'll be there in a minute."

The deputy did as she was told and escorted Riley out of the room. Desmond stood but didn't try to go after her. His brother was looking at him with an expression he couldn't read, a rarity between the Nash siblings.

"What is it?"

Declan shut the door behind him. Then he was all big brother.

"I'm not one for victim blaming so don't you go putting that on me after I say this," he started. "But I want to be a friendly reminder that she might be nice, funny and quick on her feet but the fact remains that you don't know Riley or her sister. None of us do. Not really."

Desmond felt his defenses flare.

"What are you trying to say, Dec? Do you think she's behind this?"

"No, what I'm saying is that there's something weird going on here. Brett Calder attacks her at random, you save her and then less than a month later you get her away from Geordi Green. Then, on the night you two decide to go out, *her* ex-husband is a part of some bizarre scene at *your* foundation's construction site." Declan made two fists. He shook one. "You—" He shook the other.

"And her—" He put those two fists against each other. "Keep colliding together. And I don't know why or how it keeps happening. Or who might be helping make it happen."

Desmond readied to combat whatever his brother was trying to say when Declan's expression softened. He placed one of his large hands on Desmond's shoulder and squeezed.

"All I'm saying is you can let that heart of yours do what it wants, just make sure that head sticks around too. Okay?"

Desmond nodded, holding back the staggering need to puff his chest out and fight for Riley's innocence.

"Okay," he said, instead.

"Jenna met Ryan Alcaster right out of college."

Riley was standing across from the two-way window and trying not to look at a man she, quite frankly, despised.

Declan and Desmond had come in but had given her space. Desmond was leaning against the wall next to the door, facing her, while Declan was in a chair with a notepad next to the window.

He looked up from his writing, brow raised.

"I thought we were talking about Evan Davies?"

Riley sighed. She wished she could melt into the floor and forget every ounce of the story she was about to tell.

"We are but I can't tell you about my ex-husband without talking about hers." Riley glanced at Desmond, then she let the look fall to the floor. A consequence of how much she disliked all of what she was about to say. Still, there were much worse things than telling a story.

She could have lived through Jenna's side.

"Ryan Alcaster is the CFO of Macklin Tech, a company out of Atlanta that deals in technology revolving around memory cards and external hard drives. A business model that's a dime a dozen, if you ask me, but since I've known of it Macklin seems to have been doing really well. So, whatever it is they're doing, it's working." She cleared her throat. "Anyway, right before Jenna and Ryan met, I met Davies. When we first started dating, we were both struggling to find jobs within our fields. We were considering leaving Atlanta to save some money but then Ryan got Davies a job interview at Macklin. He and Ryan had become fast friends. Ryan honestly became like a mentor too. It was a friendship that connected to their careers. Davies was hired at Macklin within the year, and just as I was about to start my online marketing freelance business, he convinced me to take an office manager job there too." Riley shrugged. "Not where I wanted my career to go but bills don't care all about that. Plus, I really thought we were lucky. We got married and then became the married couple in the office. Sure, the commute was bad but at least I had a partner in it."

Desmond shifted his weight to his other leg. Pen scratched across paper as Declan kept up with his notes. The sound of the AC kicking on created a constant background noise. Riley continued, not meeting either of their gazes.

"It wasn't until Jenna had Hartley that Macklin Tech opened a second location in Kilwin," she continued. "Nothing on the scale of the Atlanta office but strategically placed to work on a different region of the South. At least that's what I was told. What it meant for Jenna was that she had to move with Ryan to Kilwin while Davies was promoted and we stayed in Atlanta. Again, not ideal, but Jenna and I kept in touch. We video chatted daily, spoke on the phone when we had the time and still managed to feel close... But then things changed."

Riley rubbed her thumb across the knuckle of her index finger. She was actively trying not to make a fist.

"Jenna stopped wanting to video chat and then the phone calls stopped a little while after that. It was like pulling teeth to get ahold of her. I started to worry but Davies convinced me it was just Jenna getting used to being a mom and living in a new city. He convinced me to give her space. So, I did. But then one day she showed up at my door. She was acting weird and I couldn't place it until I saw the bruise on her back."

"Ryan was abusing her," Desmond said. His voice had gone cold.

It matched how Riley felt at remembering.

She nodded.

"She brushed it off in the end. Worried that it was her fault and then citing our parents as a reason for why she had to stay."

"Your parents?"

Riley finally met Desmond's blue eyes.

"We had a really good childhood and our parents often said that was because of their healthy marriage and respect for each other. It gave us stability."

"And she thought if she left Ryan that it would hurt Hartley," he guessed.

Again Riley nodded.

"She went back home and I tried to convince her for weeks to leave. When she finally told me to stop or she would get a new number, I backed off and that night I sat Davies down." That cold, hollow feeling was replaced by red-hot resentment and disbelief, even now. Riley turned to face the man she'd made an oath to stay with until death did them part. How foolish she'd been. "I guess I should have realized that me not telling him up until then was because a part of me didn't trust him. But I didn't know what to do anymore so I told him. I was *so* worried about how he would react. I was shaking. Ryan was his friend, his mentor, the reason in part for his success. Outing Ryan endangered everything Davies had worked for. But do you know what happened when I told him?"

Riley directed this to Desmond. She couldn't stand to look at the man of the story anymore.

Desmond's face was impassive.

He knew it was a rhetorical question.

Still, she paused for effect. She wanted— *needed*—someone else to feel an ounce of the impact of what had happened next.

"I didn't see any surprise in his eyes. It was that moment, that *exact* moment that I stopped loving Evan Davies."

Desmond waited a moment before he spoke. Riley didn't realize how worked up she'd become. Her breathing was faster. Harder. Angrier.

Somehow she knew Desmond felt it too. He might not have lived it but he understood the heat. The life-altering moment. The thing that cannot ever be undone.

The end of something.

Something that should have been much more.

"He knew," Desmond said, words soft. "He knew Ryan was abusing Jenna."

Riley nodded. Everything in her felt clenched.

"He told me that even though she was my twin, my sister, that that didn't give me the right to meddle in her marriage. Their problems were *their* problems. I would have filed for divorce the next day had I not gotten a call from the hospital in Kilwin. Apparently when Jenna moved there she changed her emergency contacts to me only. I flew out that night and got a hotel. The next morning I took my bruised and broken sister to the house of her abuser and helped her get everything we could before Ryan got home."

"And what did Ryan do about that?" Declan's voice was angry.

"He had a lawyer, a man who talked really fast and had a lot of expensive suits. He made a deal with Jenna. Ryan would let her keep all of her belongings and have custody of Hartley as long as she kept her mouth shut about the abuse. If not, he'd destroy her during their divorce. Take Hartley and leave her with nothing." Both men growled in displeasure. "She agreed. That's when she came to Overlook. She could afford the move and it was quiet. I stayed in Atlanta to get all of my ducks in a row and came out here once my divorce was finalized."

Riley pointed to the two-way window. Davies continued to stare at his cup, unaware of the emotional roller coaster three people were going through that he had helped cause in the other room.

"Davies tried to get ahold of me several times after that but I changed my number. No one other than my parents even knows I'm living with Jenna. *He* shouldn't be here."

Desmond pushed off the wall. He walked over to Riley and stood so close that their arms touched. He stared through the window with palpable anger.

"Then let's find out why he is," he said. "So we can get him the hell out."

Chapter Eleven

Evan Davies was taller than Desmond. Obviously using the gym on a regular basis, he had a lean but strong build. His Facebook profile picture showed a carefree-looking man too. Messy hair but groomed beard trimmed short, his expression midlaugh and dark eyes with crinkles at the sides.

Engaging.

Harmless.

He could hold his own in a tussle.

That was the impression Desmond would have drawn of the man under different circumstances.

Yet, as it was in Davies's case, looks had most definitely been deceiving.

"I'm not talking without a lawyer."

Davies had been singing that song since Declan walked into the room. Singing it without meeting his gaze once. He paid devout attention to the drink he'd been given and the cuffs holding him to the table. Those lines at the sides of his eyes that were earned by laughter had all smoothed out. That smile from his picture had sunk low.

Any power his physique offered had been lost in the curve of his hunched-over stance.

Desmond wasn't a fan.

Every aspect of the tight-lipped man spoke of cowardice and guilt.

At least, that's how Desmond felt as he watched Declan try to get Davies to rescind his request for a lawyer or just give them any clue as to what was going on.

No dice.

He kept his head down and what he knew to himself.

It was infuriating.

It had a mixed effect in the viewing room.

Riley had gone just as tight-lipped. Desmond kept muttering beneath his breath, unable to keep his anger at bay. This man knew and possibly had a hand in what had happened to Marty, a good man who had only been trying to help Desmond. Based on that fact alone, Desmond was upset. Add to it the fact that he was Riley's ex-husband and just so happened to be in the same town where she was currently living?

Was he stalking her?

And, if so, why was he at Second Wind? He couldn't have known they'd show up, right?

It was driving Desmond crazy that he couldn't get any answers.

If not for him, at least for Riley.

Declan gave up after it was clear Davies wasn't

going to say a word more. He kept his composure until he was in the viewing room. There he swore before he addressed them.

"I'm sorry I couldn't get anything. Though I'm not surprised after what we now know about him. He's good at keeping his mouth shut." Riley didn't tear her eyes away from the two-way mirror but Desmond watched her expression at Declan's words. Her jaw tightened. "We'll keep working this whole thing to see if we can't find our own bread crumbs that can lead us somewhere that makes sense, but as for that jerk in there? We're waiting out his lawyer who's supposed to be here in the morning."

"What happens until then?" It was the first time Riley had spoken since the big reveal of her past. Desmond couldn't claim to know her as well as the man she so clearly despised in the room across from them but he could tell something was off with her.

Not surprising, considering.

She sounded different.

"He'll go into one of our cells downstairs," Declan answered. "We have enough to hold him for now." Riley nodded, curt. "As for you two, you're free to go. I just need to talk to Des about something really quickly."

"Would it be okay if I wait outside?" she asked, looking up at Desmond. "I could use some air."

"Yeah, sure." He gave his brother a questioning

look while passing Riley his keys. "I don't think she needs to be alone right now," he told Declan once Riley was out of earshot.

"I know, but I didn't want to say this in front of her."

Declan moved them to the wall, away from the closest deputy's desk.

"This doesn't leave the room," he prefaced. "You understand?"

It was the sheriff talking.

Desmond nodded.

"Understood."

Declan didn't whisper but he didn't have his normal volume either.

"Brett Calder is dead."

"What?" Desmond felt his eyebrows go sky-high. "How? I thought he was locked up?"

"He was," Declan confirmed. "And that's where he was killed, by an inmate. A fight in the yard is what I've been told. When you called earlier, I was talking to the warden."

"The warden? Of Jones Correctional?" Desmond asked, doing fast math in his head. "Isn't that an hour away?" There was no way Declan had gone out there considering his response time to Desmond's second call from the construction site.

"He came here."

"To tell you Brett Calder was killed," Desmond

deadpanned. That didn't seem like normal protocol.

"It wasn't as much that he was killed as who he was killed by and what they found after."

"Okay…"

Declan sighed.

"A man with a scorpion tattoo killed him, and while trying to save him, the doctor on call found the same scorpion tattoo on Brett."

Desmond understood why he was being told the news in private now.

Scorpion tattoos meant…

"Brett was a Fixer?"

Fixer wasn't the official title of the up-and-coming criminal organization that was based out of Kilwin, but it was the easiest description of what the men and women with the scorpion tattoos did. They were contractors, hired by gangs and less-than-desirables to do the too-difficult jobs or the ones that were just too messy to risk. And, when all else failed, they seemed to be the best at fixing whatever their clients had done wrong.

The Nash family knew of their existence thanks to two Fixers who had targeted Madi the year before at the behest of one very angry man.

"My best guess is that he was a new recruit," Declan said. "And not a good one at that. But I do think that the man who killed him was sent into that place to do just that. I think the Fixers took a hit out on him because of how public his attack on Riley was. Not to mention he was caught, not something that group looks kindly upon."

"The man Riley spoke to at the construction site, the one in the nice suit, you think he's one of them?"

The Fixers were also known for their business ensembles. Madi had been attacked by well-dressed men.

"I'm not ruling it out, but Riley saw his face and he let her leave. He also didn't take or destroy her phone after she dropped it." Declan shrugged. "As morbid as it is to say, that concerns me. If he is a Fixer, I don't know what the current job they're running is but it can't be good."

Desmond knew his brother didn't mean he was concerned because Riley was okay. He was concerned because none of their pieces were matching up. They took a moment to scowl at one another, both lost in their own thoughts. Desmond found another question.

"Why did the warden come to you? Couldn't he have just called and told you?"

Declan's expression softened.

"He's an old friend of Dad's. He knew that Brett had pushed the family back into the spotlight and correctly assumed his death would probably do it again, especially with the mention of the Fixers. He wanted to give me a heads-up in person."

Desmond couldn't help but smile a little.

"Dad's been gone for years and still he finds ways to help us out."

Declan didn't smile but he did agree.

The conversation ended with promises to talk more in the morning after Davies's lawyer came in. Declan gave Desmond a quick embrace, no doubt softened by the mention of their father, and disappeared into his office.

The night air hit Desmond's body as he pushed outside into the cold. He was surprised to see Riley leaning against the passenger's-side door instead of sitting inside the truck. He liked walking out into the cold but he didn't know if he would have been lounging in it. Riley turned her head toward him as he moved into the parking lot. She made no move to open the door. Desmond redirected from the driver's side and stopped in front of her.

He could smell lavender. He could also see she was chewing on saying something. Her brow was creased and her eyes had a cut to them. Desmond couldn't tell what emotion she was dancing on.

"You okay?"

Riley nodded. Then she shook her head. Dark, enchanting eyes found his. When she spoke, Desmond felt like it was the only sound for miles.

"I was happy, married and had a plan for the future. Then I blinked. Suddenly I was angry, divorced and just trying to hold on to some semblance of what my normal was. Then I blinked again and I was here, in Overlook. Happier, and then, the moment I started to think about making new plans, I became a victim. Then I was someone who was saved. But, I know I was lucky. It could have been so much worse and I promise I'm not upset about any of that. It was a speed bump on an already bumpy road so it wasn't that big of a deal. But then? I blinked." She shrugged. Her words were raw. "My ex-husband is in there because of God knows what he did. He shouldn't be here. This is my new life. My new normal. He's not supposed to be in that. And, Desmond, he's a smart man. Resourceful and cunning when needed. What was he doing at the construction site? Who was the man in the suit? How am I going to tell Jenna any of this without bringing up all the bad stuff that happened? And did Davies do that to Marty? How was I married to him? What does that say about me?"

Her words had quickened, her chest rising with an emotional cadence. Desmond acted on instinct. Riley's cheek was smooth and cold against the palm of his hand. The space between them all but disappeared. He tilted her head up. Those beautiful eyes were glossed over with pain, fear, confusion.

He knew the group well.

"It says that you're living your life the way it should be lived," he said with a genuine, if not small, smile. "It means you fell in love, you trusted, you took a chance, you survived, and now you have the luxury of questioning what the future may bring. Life was never meant to be easy, just as it is never promised that it would always be hard. We'll figure out what's going on. Together. I promise, okay?"

Riley's voice was soft but she nodded.

"Okay."

"Okay," he repeated.

Desmond dropped his hand, but he didn't step back.

Instead he glanced at the painted red lips of Riley Stone.

He didn't have time for a lot of things, but a kiss? He could make time for that.

However, those same lips he was imaging against his turned up into a smile. She was trying not to laugh. It earned a skeptical grin from him.

"What?"

"I was just thinking, you asked how I was and I didn't really give a solid answer," she said. "What I *should* have said was *hungry*. I'm guessing the Red Oak isn't open after midnight, huh?"

Desmond laughed. He finally put space between them again.

"No, it's definitely closed." He held up his index finger. "But. If you're up for it, I know someone who makes the *best* PB&Js this side of the Mississippi."

Riley's eyebrow arced up, dangerously close to playful. It made Desmond regret their bodies no longer touching. To his surprise she nodded before he explained.

"I'm in."

DECLAN, CALEB AND his wife, Desmond's mother and Desmond all lived full-time on the ranch at the end of Winding Road. Yet as they had driven down the paved road through the ranch, Riley hadn't been able to tell.

Everything was quiet. Peaceful.

Now, sitting across from Desmond at his dining-room table, that feeling of contentment had come inside with them.

"You weren't kidding about the best peanut-butter-and-jelly sandwiches," she said after finishing hers off. Desmond was working on his second one already. He shrugged.

"What can I say? I am a man of specific talents." He flashed her what Riley could only describe as a "winning" smile. It brightened the man; it brightened the room. It made *her* feel bright.

"You know, you have the strangest way of making me feel better," she blurted out. Instantly she felt heat in her cheeks. She hurried on. "*What I mean* is I get why everyone roots for you. You help people and seem to genuinely enjoy it."

Desmond waved off the compliment.

"I'm only doing what anyone would in my situation."

Riley scoffed.

"You have money, enough I feel like you could do whatever you wanted. Or, at least, very close to it." She motioned to the house around them. "But here you are. Living a stone's throw away from your mom and in a town you could have left and never come back to. What's more, you didn't have to start Second Wind. But you did. You must enjoy the work or just really enjoy the attention."

Desmond's smile faltered.

It softened Riley.

"And I don't think you Nashes have the luxury here to crave any attention," she added on, gentle.

"No, we get that in spades already."

Riley could have turned the conversational tide. She could have complimented his house—modern rustic, white, black, gray and wood and somehow perfect for the cowboy—or asked about the assortment of books she could see, or listened to an urge that had been simmering since he'd noticeably looked down at her lips outside the sheriff's department and fly across the table and rock his world.

Yet, she stayed the course, her curiosity finally too loud to ignore.

"Why *did* you start Second Wind?"

Chapter Twelve

Desmond put his half-eaten sandwich down. Riley worried she'd overstepped but then his expression turned thoughtful. A clock somewhere in the house ticked off a rhythm. The heat had turned on when they'd first stepped through the front door. Both of their jackets were draped over the couch in the living room.

And now Riley was going to learn another answer about the illustrious Desmond Nash.

"When I was a kid I was given the unique perspective of living through a trauma," he started. "To say it changed me is an understatement. It changed all of us Nashes. Even the town." Riley tried to keep her face impassive but Desmond gave her a knowing look. "I'm assuming you've heard about the real reason everyone knows the Nash name around Overlook?"

"I read about it during the coverage after what happened the night of the gala," she admitted.

Desmond didn't seem at all bothered, or surprised, but Riley still felt shame heating her cheeks.

"The Nash triplet abduction carries a fame all its own around here. The greatest unsolved mystery in Overlook. The tragedy that shook a community to its core. The family who was forever broken when three eight-year-olds sneaked out to the park alone. I've seen and heard several versions of the story, but there's a few things the papers and gossip mill never got quite right." He smiled but it disappeared quickly. "Madi's scream when the man grabbed her with a gun in his hand is the worst sound I've heard to this day. Sometimes I still hear it when my dreams get bad. Caleb once said it was like the trees came alive long enough to scream with her. It's a sound that will always, always haunt us."

Riley wanted to reach out but held off. Desmond was ramping up to a point. She just needed to hang on for the ride and listen.

"They also usually mess up the next part. At least, I've heard several versions of what happened," he continued. "What *really* happened was Madi fought back against the man. She took her tiny fist and hit his throat as hard as she could. Honestly, if she had been older, *bigger*, I think the move would have helped us. But, we were only eight so it just ticked him off. He pistol-whipped Madi, knocked her out cold and then he shot at Caleb and me. The bullet hit Caleb's arm." Riley gasped. That hadn't been in the paper. Desmond touched his biceps. "It was just a graze but at the time all I saw was blood. So much of it. I just—" Up until then his voice had been consistent. He was telling a story in a concise and even way. Now, though, there was an invisible ripple that seemed to move across him.

Tension hardened his shoulders. His jaw tightened. His nostrils flared. He took the smallest of moments to, well, she didn't know what. But Riley let him be. She had already pushed as much as she was going to push.

When Desmond was ready again there was no denying the anger in his words. Deep, boundless anger.

"I lost it. Every part of me snapped. My family was in trouble. I *had* to help. Or at least try." He shifted his leg under the table. The one with the limp. "We jumped on the man's back but it wasn't enough to do much damage. He threw me to the ground and stomped on my leg until it nearly shattered. After that, Caleb was the only one left standing. He made a decision. He wouldn't escape, he wouldn't fight. He'd instead do as the man said to stay with Madi and me. So, that's how we ended up in the basement of Well Water Cabin."

The name bothered him.

It bothered *her* and she wasn't even a part of it.

"The man kept us in the basement apartment

for three days. He brought us food, only spoke to threaten us and then disappeared."

"Your leg was broken," Riley had to reiterate. "Did that bother him?"

Desmond shook his head. She could tell he was caught in the memory.

"He didn't seem bothered by any of it, but, then we initiated our plan and he seemed to care about that."

Riley couldn't help but lean a little closer. Her heart hurt for the then children. For that to happen to anyone was terrifying but to be young children too? Riley wouldn't wish that on anyone.

"I was really sick by the third day. We all knew I needed help. And soon. We had to do something or we ran the very real risk of me dying there. So we decided to pretend like I'd stopped breathing since I already looked like death as it was. Caleb and Madi cried and screamed and, I think, forgot that it wasn't actually true. That I was alive. Regardless it was convincing. The man came in, bent over me to check my pulse, and then the triplet power kicked in."

On that he gave a small smile.

"Triplet power?" she had to ask.

"It's what Declan called it. Basically everything after that became a blur for us. We acted as a unit, as a team. We weren't three kids anymore, we were a hive mind. We overpowered the man, managed to lock the door behind us and escaped into the woods and found help. I went to the hospital and Caleb showed everyone where we had been held."

"And no one found the man."

"And no one found the man," he repeated. "And no one found out why he'd done it in the first place or what the endgame had been. My father, a detective at the time, tried. He ran that case into the ground for years. His determination became an obsession. One that built up years and years of stress until it finally made his heart give out."

Riley shook her head, sorrow ringing through her for the man sitting across the table and all that he'd endured.

Desmond surprised her with a chuckle.

"So I guess my answer to your original question of why I started Second Wind is less lengthy." The strain of the story started to fall away. He relaxed into his chair again. "We survived what happened but I realized that was only one part of the battle. To find life again, to *live* life again, was in some ways harder. After I got lucky from investments I'd made during college, I opened a series of nonprofits but realized as well-intentioned as I was, hiring experts and others who had the degrees and training to help was more in my wheelhouse. That's when I had the idea to start a foundation that sought out nonprofits and groups who work with helping people who have lived through trauma and tragedy find new life again. A place that could help others *help others*."

"To find their second wind," Riley realized.

Desmond nodded.

"Not the most clever of names but I'm proud of it."

He was back. Back to the present. Back to a smile. His story was over.

"You *should* be proud," Riley said. She meant it.

Desmond finished off his sandwich and took both of their plates to the kitchen. Riley stood and stretched. She was tired, she knew that, but also there was a restlessness there. One that made the thought of going home leave a bad taste in her mouth.

Maybe it was all the adrenaline that had coursed through her earlier that night, the fear and anguish at what had happened to Marty. Maybe it was the sudden reappearance of Davies and the worry that he'd come to town for her. Maybe it was the memory of kissing Desmond, a knee-jerk reaction that was, admittedly, leaving a long-lasting impression.

Did Riley want to do it again? Now that Davies was back, heralding in every memory of the bad that had happened in the last year, was there any room left in her to want that?

Riley felt her cheeks heat and was aware of a pulse of longing below her waistline, letting her head know that her body certainly wanted to be closer to Desmond.

She spun around on her heel, worried he'd see the no doubt glaring blush against her pale skin, and walked across the hardwood floor to the living room. The house around them was a large two-story but the living area was much more cozy. A deep-cushioned couch sat opposite a flat-screen TV while a bookcase took up most of the wall between the two. Knickknacks, picture frames and other pieces of decor were dispersed among the books, making the room feel even more like a home.

Riley ran her finger across one of the shelves as she danced her gaze between the pictures.

Almost every picture Desmond was in, there was at least one sibling with him. High school and college graduations, birthdays with three kids around one cake, Declan being sworn in as sheriff, a few candids from the dance floor of what looked like two different weddings, a worn picture of Dorothy and Michael Nash smiling and hugging and a group picture of the Nash siblings and their significant others. Riley got hung up on that one a little longer than the rest. Desmond and Declan had no one by their sides.

The last picture was of just Desmond. He was on a beautiful white-and-brown-patched horse, his black Stetson perched atop his head and a wry grin across his lips.

"Winona." Riley jumped; Desmond laughed. "Sorry, I thought you heard me," he said, moving level with her. He motioned to the picture. "That's my horse Winona. I think if you looked up the word *wild* in the dictionary there would be a picture of her there staring at you."

Riley snorted.

"I'd bet Hartley sans a nap would be there too," she added in. "I've found that a sleepy nephew is a terrifying nephew." At that Riley checked the time on her phone. It was almost one in the morning. She'd already updated Jenna about what had happened after giving her official statement at the sheriff's department. She'd also texted Jenna that she was headed to Desmond's house. That text had been met with a series of large-eyes emojis and the teasing reminder to use protection.

There was no way Riley could sneak in without waking both the grumpy beast and the woman who had created him.

Riley shared a look with the man next to her.

This time it was her who was guilty of looking at his lips.

She sighed.

"How competitive are you?"

The question caught Riley completely off guard. And that was saying something considering their night.

"Excuse me?"

Desmond swept his arm toward the TV.

"Ma preaches stress-free living but when it comes to *Wheel of Fortune*, not only does she force me to DVR it, she challenges me to solve the puzzle before her." His eyebrow raised, completely playful. "Want to go a round before I take you home?"

Riley didn't think twice.

"Only if you don't mind losing."

DESMOND OPENED HIS eyes slowly.

Something was wrong. He wasn't where he was supposed to be.

The world didn't look the same as it had during the night.

He blinked, confused.

Then he saw white shiplap.

It was his ceiling. He knew because that shiplap had been a big deal to his sister and Mom. They'd seen it on a show and thought it was trendy. He'd caved and, though he'd never admit it to them, enjoyed the look.

But he couldn't piece together why he was seeing it.

Then he saw red.

That's when the haze of sleep lifted.

He was in the living room, on the couch, lying on his back, and he wasn't alone.

Riley was tucked into his side, head on his shoulder and an arm and a leg draped over him. He tilted his chin down to get a better look at their situation. She wasn't just on him; he had his arm around her too. Holding her.

In their sleep.

Desmond replayed the last waking memory he had.

They had watched an episode of *Wheel of Fortune* and made it a competitive affair. Riley had solved two of the four phrases and was raring to beat his two wins during the next episode. Yet, as the commercial break came on, she had quieted. By the time Pat was introducing the contestants she had nodded off against him.

Desmond had fully intended on waking her and taking her home, but looking down at her face, lax in sleep, something in him had softened. Riley had been through a lot just in the last twenty-four hours. He could let her sleep for a few minutes.

So, he'd grabbed the throw blanket next to him, put it around her and tried to guess the Thing or Place that had three *G*s but no *A*s.

Apparently, past that, things hadn't gone according to plan.

The TV had turned itself off because of the lack of activity for, he assumed, hours and the living room was bathed in light from the front windows behind the couch.

Desmond sat still for a moment, perplexed.

Before the night of the gala he didn't have time

for distractions. After the run through the woods? He still didn't have the time for distractions.

But now?

The distraction against him was warm and smelled like lavender.

Riley Stone had the intelligence and courage to think on her feet and act with compassion.

Desmond had had his fair share of dates and relationships before he'd come back to Overlook full-time. He'd been attracted to women of all shapes and sizes. Yet, there was something all of them had been missing. Something he couldn't quite put into words.

Lying there, beneath the shiplap, in the sunlight, and with a mass of dark red curls against his chest, Desmond couldn't help but think Riley Stone might just have that *something* he'd been looking for.

He smiled, weirdly calm about the idea, when the woman in question started to stir. Desmond froze but Riley kept moving. Her body shifted farther on top of him. He couldn't stop a grunt at the new position.

The noise must have gotten through to her.

It was Riley's turn to freeze in place.

For a moment no one moved.

Then the red curls shifted. Desmond met a dark, widened gaze with a hopefully impassive expression.

Riley was less quiet about their predicament.

"Oh my God."

Desmond groaned again as Riley did her best impression of an acrobat. She tried to jump off him but went into a sort of roll. Desmond, imaging the coffee table not too far from the couch, scrambled to stop her.

In the end all their actions did was land them both on the floor.

This time it was Desmond on top. He moved his knees on either side of her body to keep his weight off and sat up on his elbows.

Riley, face as red as a cherry, stared up at him without saying a word.

Desmond couldn't help it.

He grinned.

Then, to his undeniable pleasure, Riley burst into laughter.

"JENNA IS NEVER going to believe me," Riley said after she could breathe again.

Desmond grinned. His eyebrow raised so slow it was absolutely devilish. In the daylight he was less of the closed-up businessman and reminded her more of a mischievous teenager. Or maybe that was Riley putting a sneaking-around, trying-not-to-get-caught-by-their-parents vibe to their current situation.

Desmond Nash was literally on top of her.

And she'd be remiss if she didn't acknowledge that she didn't hate it.

"What wouldn't she believe?" His voice didn't help matters. The smooth baritone had become husky.

It was all Riley could do to keep her own from quavering.

"That we fell asleep on the couch watching *Wheel of Fortune*," she said with another bite of laughter. "It sounds like a lie waiting to happen."

Desmond chuckled. Riley felt it against her entire body.

"Or sounds like a pretty poor way to woo a woman."

Riley shrugged against the rug. Her mortification at waking up on top of the cowboy had turned into fast laughter. Now that urge transformed into a smile and a tease.

"Hey, it *did* get me to sleep with you, didn't it?"

Riley was pretty sure she could heat an entire hot tub with the blush scorching her body, but at the same time, she was leaning into the awkward.

Yet, her little joke didn't seem to land. In fact, the cowboy's expression had gone in the opposite direction of humor. His brow creased, those light blue eyes homed in and his smile vanished.

Then it was like a switch flipped.

The heat of embarrassment was gone. In its place was a different heat. One that she hadn't felt in a long time, marriage included if she was being completely honest.

The kind of heat that made your entire body

stand at attention. The kind of heat that made you acutely aware of every breath you took, how high your chest rose along with it and how your body had already made up its mind about what it wanted to do next.

When Desmond's eyes trailed down to her lips, Riley had already been prepared for his kiss for what felt like an eternity.

Chapter Thirteen

If looking at the cowboy was a stimulating event, kissing him was nearly downright debilitating.

Riley had no room between Desmond and the floor to sigh in relief at finally being kissed by him. But she did have the space to moan against his lips as his tongue parted hers.

In the back of her head Riley couldn't help but blanch at the fact that it was morning and she'd just woken up which meant her breath probably wasn't the best. She wasn't charmed out of the realization that Desmond also probably needed a stick of gum or a swig of mouthwash.

Yet, as their kiss deepened, Riley couldn't fault a thing.

She wound her arms around his neck and held on as he maneuvered for a better position. Dropping down onto one elbow, Desmond angled his body so he was on his side and she was pressed against him. It gave her more room to move.

When he grabbed her hip, she pushed toward him.

When that hand went up the back of her shirt, she moved hers to the hem of his.

When his bare skin slid between her shoulder blades, trailing heat and a wonderful tingling sensation, she tugged the man's shirt up to let him know that she wanted more. For both of them.

Desmond broke the kiss but only to listen to her unasked request. He performed nothing short of a miracle by unbuttoning his shirt one-handed and with speedy precision. Riley started to pull her own shirt up, ready to throw it into oblivion, when a sound that didn't match the mood rocketed through the house around them.

It was the doorbell.

Both of them froze.

Riley took the tiniest of moments to note that Desmond wasn't wearing an undershirt. His button up was opened to reveal the muscled body of a man who might have been strolling through the business world the last several years but was also an active, active man.

Riley was still holding on to the hope that whoever was at the front door would leave before another ring so she could learn the feel of that body when another sound dashed any and all hopes of the show continuing.

It was a laugh.

A very specific laugh.

A *Jenna* laugh.

"Oh my gosh, I think that's my sister," Riley

whispered. "How did she even know where to find me? She hasn't been here before."

Desmond, who up until that point had been a cool cucumber, lost his chilled composure.

The doorbell rang again.

He swore.

"Ten bucks she's with my mother."

Riley could have medaled at how quickly she went from pressed against a good-looking man to army crawling to the hallway, out of view from the living-room windows and the front door. She didn't know how Desmond and his opened shirt reacted—it was every man and woman for themselves in her opinion—but the moment she was out of sight, Riley popped up and started smoothing her blouse. There was no hope for her hair, and she knew that, but she ran her hand across her face like it would wipe away any evidence that she'd just woken up and also just done a whole lot of making out.

"Hey," Desmond whispered. He moved to her side with speed and pulled her through the other entry into the kitchen. "The longer we don't answer, the worse it's going to be."

Riley eyed him up and down and gave a nervous snort.

"Your buttons are messed up on your shirt," she pointed out. "And your lips are as red as red can be."

Desmond turned a critical eye down to his

shirt. He attempted to rebutton it with a glance her way. The corner of his lips quirked up.

"Speaking of really red lips."

Riley groaned as the doorbell was replaced by a series of knocks.

"We're busted." There was humor in his defeat but Riley was stubborn. She followed him to the front door, ready to try to test her twin trickery. That thought went straight into the trash the moment Desmond opened the door wide.

Jenna was indeed on the front porch and she wasn't alone. Hartley was on her hip and a woman Riley only recognized from the media was at her side. Jenna's eyes went wide as she took the two of them in. A smile she was losing the struggle to hide split her face. The older woman next to her was a bit more gracious with hers. It was small but definitely there.

"Hey, Ma," Desmond greeted. "What can I do you for?"

Riley felt the flames of embarrassment kick right back up. She was pretty sure she'd done more blushing in one morning than she had in all of her years of life.

Dorothy Nash was in a set of floral-print overalls, work boots, and was sporting a tight braid draped over her shoulder. She looked like she belonged in a gardening edition of *Southern Living* magazine. Friendly, approachable and warm. Yet when she spoke there was nothing but a clever bite to her words.

It was instantly endearing to Riley. Even if it added to the lava-level blush.

"Well, *son*, a few of us have been trying to get ahold of you two and haven't had any luck. So when this wonderful young woman and her strapping young son turned up just after nine, I thought it was a great idea to come and make sure you two were okay. Maybe just interrupt a breakfast y'all forgot to tell anyone about." Her eyes shifted down. Riley followed them and almost died on the spot. Desmond had completely skipped a button on his shirt. "Clearly y'all just lost track of time and forgot to check in."

"We were watching *Wheel of Fortune* and fell asleep," Riley blurted out.

Jenna finally lost it.

"Is that what they're calling it these days?" she teased around her laughter.

"Jenna Mae," Riley screeched, now one hundred percent certain she was about to melt away.

"Riley Lee," she yelled back.

Dorothy chuckled. Desmond sighed. Riley was already moving toward the car.

"You know, I think it's time we leave. So sorry for the—the inconvenience," she said to Dorothy. "Honestly, it was just a little oversight. We'll just go ahead and get out of your hair now." Jenna could *not* stop laughing. Riley couldn't wait to go home and give her a piece of her mind.

"Hey, wait!"

Both women stopped in their tracks. Desmond disappeared into the house only to reappear a few seconds later with Riley's purse and jacket.

"Wow, it was so good you were just going to leave all of your things," Jenna whispered at her ear. Riley swatted at her.

Desmond wasn't smirking when he walked the distance she had managed to create between them and the front porch but he wasn't frowning either. He seemed amused.

Which somehow made everything worse.

"Yeah, uh, I guess I might need these," Riley said with a laugh that wasn't helping. "Thank you. And thank you for the sandwiches."

Desmond nodded.

"My pleasure."

Jenna made a noise but Riley wasn't having it. She smiled at Hartley, the only innocent one out of them, and took Jenna's elbow.

"Ms. Stone?"

Both Riley and Jenna turned again. This time it was the Nash matriarch who had spoken. She addressed Riley as she continued.

"Tonight is our weekly family dinner. I sure would love it if you three could come." She smiled. The skin next to her eyes crinkled. "It's been a while since we've had new faces around the table."

Riley started to cycle through a few reasons why she didn't want to accept—mostly it was just embarrassment at being caught like a couple of guilty teens—but, once again, Jenna took action.

"We'd *love* to," she called back. "Just tell us a time and we'll be here with bells on!"

Riley found Desmond's gaze. He sighed and rubbed the back of his neck, now annoyed. She worried that her sister had done that, but just as quickly as he looked ready to roll his eyes, he was smirking again.

Riley focused on those lips.

The ones she'd just gotten *very* well acquainted with.

The same set that she couldn't help but hope to touch again.

"Five-thirty. Five if you'd like to see this one here take a ride on his horse."

"Mom," Desmond complained.

She ignored it.

"That sounds *perfect*," Jenna said. "See you then!"

Riley finally got her escape. It wasn't until they were in the car and pointed toward Winding Road that she warned her sister.

"Not a word, Jenna. I mean it."

Jenna, of course, didn't listen.

"This isn't ideal."

It was nearing four in the afternoon and Desmond was about to point out to Caleb that what he'd just said was one hell of an understatement.

What wasn't *ideal* was having your mother show up on your front porch and effectively catching you in the act of getting *close* with someone.

What wasn't *ideal* was having that same mother bebop around your house, peppering you with questions about your intentions, your *feelings* and your future goals in relation to the young woman you so obviously spent that close time with.

What wasn't *ideal* was, after finally getting your nosy mother out of your hair, starting to ask yourself all of those things only to be interrupted by news that was so far from ideal it was laughable.

"Evan Davies being let go less than twenty-four hours after he was arrested is a travesty of justice," Desmond decided. "Way worse than not ideal."

Caleb let out a long breath. He nodded.

"Hey, I'm not thrilled about it either but the department's hands are tied. That lawyer of his was no joke. Once Marty came to and said it was the man in the suit who knocked him out and he hadn't even seen Davies, there wasn't much we could do."

They were standing in the stable between both of their horses. Winona was ready to go on their daily ride while Ax, Caleb's overo, was tired after returning from his. Both men were out of their work clothes and in outfits they'd probably wear every day for the rest of their natural lives. Button-down flannels, Levi's jeans, boots and their Stetsons. There wasn't a stitch of clothes that they were more comfortable in than what was worn as they'd grown up, working the ranch.

"His story made no sense." Desmond thought that was worth repeating. "He came to town to check on Riley after seeing her in the paper. Then just happened to be riding past Second Wind when he saw Marty being jumped? Then when we show up he throws himself from the second story to avoid us?" Desmond growled. "He's lying."

Caleb shrugged.

"I know but that doesn't change what happened. Being weird isn't a crime and we can't prove he did anything other than that."

Desmond felt the urge to cuss someone. Seeing as he was surrounded by horses and his brother, he squashed the urge.

"Listen, we didn't just send him on his merry way," Caleb added. "Declan did his terrifying sheriff voice with a warning that it might be better if Davies just left Overlook. He might have been lying about why he was at Second Wind but you could see clear in his eyes he was going to heed Declan's words."

That didn't make the knot in Desmond's stom-

ach unclench. It also didn't erase the worry that
he knew without even hearing her that had been
in Riley's tone when Caleb had passed along the
information that Davies was free.

Desmond wasn't surprised when Caleb picked
up on his thoughts.

"Jazz and her husband followed Davies to the
town line without him even knowing. He's gone
and do you know who should be here soon?"
Caleb reverted to a grin. He answered his own
question. "The very same lady you tried to woo
with *Wheel of Fortune* and PB&Js."

The serious part of the conversation turned to
siblings jabbing at one another. Just as the Stone
sisters had on his front porch earlier that day. It
was nice to see that the pain of having siblings
wasn't a Nash-family-only event.

Caleb left to shower and Desmond took Winona out into the field. Before the abduction he
hadn't been a tried-and-true lover of riding like
Caleb and Declan. His father had always tried to
get him more enthused about it but the words always fell flat. It was like Michael Nash was trying to put an ethereal feeling into mere words.
The sentiment never moved Desmond.

Then he'd had surgery on his leg. Worries of
partially being paralyzed became worries of per-
manent nerve damage which in turn became concern that walking would never be the same for him.

Desmond remembered the suffocating feeling of being surrounded by questions, fears and worry. It had sent him on crutches out to the same field. There his father had found him. Unlike his mother, the Nash family patriarch was all blunt, all the time.

He had pointed toward the horses and then laid a heavy truth on his young son's shoulders.

"There's a chance your leg may never be the way it used to be, son. But, that doesn't mean there's not an entire world out there that you can't enjoy," he'd said. "There's never enough time to do every single thing you want to but there's *always* time to do at least one thing. You just need to make that one thing count."

The last part was Michael Nash's mantra. One that he'd told his children countless times. Desmond and Madi had never put much stock in the saying like Caleb had—to them it had just been another memory of their father they repeated to feel close—but in the last few years things had started to change for them.

There was a beauty to their father's words. One that, spoken to him in that moment when he was nine, Desmond now felt deeply as an adult.

"If you can't walk the way you want, then do something else you can," his father had continued, looking out at the horses. "And do it with everything you've got."

That's how Desmond had channeled his frustrations and fears. He'd found an outlet and new-found love for riding. Even now, what felt like a lifetime later, feeling the power of a horse beneath him, feeling the rhythm of hooves against the earth and feeling the rush of wind was second to none.

It always started the same. He was a kid again, running to reclaim a life that had almost been taken. A teen, worried about his father's obsession with their unsolved case. A young adult, mourning his father's death and scared for what it would do to the rest of the family. An adult, trying to help other families from drowning in the wake of tragedy and trauma.

Then, all at once, he was just a kid laughing in the wind. A teen who marveled at how fast he could go. A young adult who felt invincible. An adult who wished the feeling would never end.

And, sometimes, Desmond's mind relaxed enough that he could look back at that same fence he'd stood at when he was nine and see his father.

Smiling because his son finally understood.

Chapter Fourteen

Hartley was in a walking mood.

No sooner had Riley gotten him out of his car seat was he marching toward Mimi's Boutique with a purpose. Riley couldn't help but laugh as she locked the car and hurried to take his hand.

A woman was laughing too when they walked through the front door, setting off the bell over it.

"He must know what he wants," she exclaimed, looking at the one-man marching band with red curls galore.

Riley shrugged.

"I guess so! Usually he's not the best at shopping but today I guess is a good day."

The woman, a few years older and with a few more laugh lines than Riley, stayed behind the counter but motioned to the store.

"And what about his mama? Does she know what she's looking for?"

Hartley made a beeline for the first rack of clothes. Mimi's Boutique, by its name alone, seemed to be just for clothing but Jenna had assured her it was a one-stop shop for a variety of things.

Like fancy tins to put freshly baked chocolate-chip cookies in.

"Actually, his mama has a migraine so I volunteered to be on aunt duty," Riley felt the need to correct. "But this aunt is wondering where your festive but not-too-festive dessert tins are?"

The woman, who Riley knew wasn't Mimi, placed a bookmark in her current read and came around the counter with the same purpose Hartley was using to browse.

"We have just the thing."

Minutes later, and a quick introduction that led into a chat about the best recipe for rocky-road brownies, and Riley was staring down at a circular tin with a horse-ranch theme to it. A little on the nose but Riley saw it as cute. She just hoped Dorothy Nash wasn't tired of the ranch theme.

"Have fun," the woman, named Patricia, called. "See you later, handsome man!"

Both women laughed as Hartley responded with an excited, "Bye!"

"You're a rock star in your own right, did you know that?" Riley asked him as she went back to the task of buckling him into the car seat.

"I'm a stud," he exclaimed.

That got Riley really giggling.

So much so she didn't hear the man approach

her from behind. Yet when she was done and had turned around, there was no way to avoid him.

"Davies."

The first time Riley had met her ex-husband it had been a nice hot summer day. They were at a pool party and boy, had Davies been a sight. Easy on the eyes, quick with a smile and funny. He was sure of himself and confidence in Riley's peers at that age was a rare thing right out of college. It, more so than any of his other traits, drew her to him like a moth to a flame.

He knew what he wanted.

He went for it.

When it didn't happen, he readjusted.

Then went after it again.

There was a poetry to it. An infectious quality. One that had wrapped around her the more time she had spent with him.

Now?

Riley was standing in front of a man she didn't recognize.

He wore a suit, one she'd bought him as a gift for his first big promotion. At the time it had gone hand in hand with his confidence and determination. Now it looked like he'd stolen it from his father in an attempt to seem like an adult. Or, maybe, it was just him. There was a shiftiness to Davies and he looked like sleep had been eluding him for some time.

He was a ghost of his former self and it was

taking all Riley could do in that moment not to feel grief over the loss.

Evan Davies had once been a man of potential. Now he was just a man wasting away in a suit.

"Where is she?" he started, no segue or greeting.

"What?"

He lowered his voice. It, like his demeanor, was panicky.

"Where is she?"

Riley shook her head. Was he really still trying to find *her* by pestering who he thought was Jenna?

She couldn't believe it.

The nerve.

"I'm not telling you anything other than to leave this town." She angled her body so she was blocking Hartley from view. Her shoulders were squared, anger tensing her muscles.

Davies glanced toward the door of the boutique. Patricia was standing in front of the window staring.

He shifted his eyes back to Riley before averting them.

"There's a lot going on you don't understand," he said, still basically whispering. "It all— It all just keeps happening and I—" He swore. Riley wasn't afraid of Davies. Not when she knew what a coward he really was. Yet, her heartbeat did pick up speed as obvious anger washed over the man. "I'm just trying to do something right. That's—"

The bell over the door to Mimi's Boutique sounded.

"You alright?" Patricia called.

Davies's anger washed away as fast as it had come on.

"I'm sorry," he said. Then he was walking across the street.

Riley turned to Patricia. She had her phone in hand.

"You alright?" she repeated.

Riley heard the sound of a car door shut and the engine come on.

"I am now."

SOME OF THE NASH family were already at the main house when Riley pulled up. She was disappointed that Desmond wasn't among them but she did catch Declan.

"I don't think anything else will come of this but I decided I still needed to give you a heads-up, just in case," she prefaced then she told him about her run-in with Davies. He was less than pleased. Then he went and made some phone calls.

Riley felt bad for putting a scowl on his face.

Dorothy and Madi were in the second wave of Nash family that Riley spoke with. Dorothy was thrilled about the cookies and the tin, while Madi was excited to see Hartley again.

"Addison is inside playing. Maybe we can go in there too?"

It was a cool day but not downright cold. Riley wore a dark blue dress with her suede ankle boots, trying to show off clothing she'd gotten several compliments on before and shoes that made her the perfect height to kiss.

Not that she expected to be doing that but she *did* have to admit that she'd thought of no one other than a certain cowboy as she was getting ready.

"That sounds like fun! Right?"

Hartley nodded. "Yeah!"

The boy was what Jenna referred to as a true empath. If you were excited, he was excited. If you were sad, he was sad. If you wanted a cookie, he wanted a cookie.

Though Riley wasn't convinced that wasn't just a toddler thing.

The main house was a beautiful construction. Newer than Riley had expected. It was filled with warmth, brightness and walls covered in framed pictures of the family.

"I'm sorry Jenna isn't feeling well," Dorothy said after Hartley had settled into a playpen filled with toys. "She seemed so excited to see the horses."

Riley gave the woman a wry grin.

"Yes. It was the horses she was excited to see."

They shared a look. Dorothy suppressed a

laugh. They both knew it was the cowboy Jenna had been ready to drool over while simultaneously slapping Riley in the shoulder with choruses of *You made out with that* and *Do you think he'd take his shirt off if we asked?*

For that reason alone Riley had decided to come to the ranch a little after five. She didn't want to be awkward standing and staring at the fence line waiting for a glimpse of what she could only assume was one heck of a good sight.

Instead of gawking, Riley spent the next few minutes talking to Dorothy and Madi about Hidden Hills, the bed-and-breakfast Madi and Julian ran. Riley found a comfortable groove with the women, despite not knowing them well. There was an ease about them. No pressure to impress, just a cruising conversation you could either ride or watch.

However, neither woman said when Desmond was coming and Riley was getting close to asking when the front door opened and the man himself walked on through.

His hair was wet, his jeans looked painted on and his baby blues went right to her. Riley felt heat move across her body. Very awkward considering her current company.

"Hey! Look!" Hartley grabbed Desmond's attention before he could make it to their group. The boy had his Mr. Puppy, a Great Dane with a cowboy hat sewn between its ears, in his hand.

Desmond stopped to inspect it. Then he was talking to the boy with such rapt attention, Riley felt her hormones rise in answer.

"Des is good with kids," Madi said at her side. "Just so you know."

Riley averted her gaze with a smile and tried to get back into the conversation, proving she could concentrate on something other than the man, but failed immediately. She couldn't help but keep an eye on the two as Desmond spent a little time playing with Hartley.

A disappointing thought moved across her chest.

What if Desmond thought she was Jenna?

Geordi had, Davies had, and who was to say he hadn't just gotten lucky that day at the park?

She couldn't blame him if so. Riley and Jenna refused to compromise on the looks they liked just because others confused the two of them. Which meant their hair was nearly the same length and, thanks to a matching metabolism and exercise routine, so was their weight. Their fashion sense went along with it and even their attempts at cat-eye eyeliner were similarly disastrous.

She took a small breath as Hartley lost interest and Desmond finally turned back to her.

He smiled.

Desmond had every right to mistake her for Jenna.

But Riley hoped he wouldn't.

"WHERE'S JENNA?" DESMOND greeted, scoping out his family's home but coming up short. Declan was outside on the phone and Caleb and Nina hadn't shown up yet. Maybe she was in the back at the grill with Julian.

Riley stepped away from her conversation with Madi and their mom and let out a noticeable exhale. Her cheeks were flushed. He was about to ask what was wrong when she smiled and answered.

"She was 'taken by a migraine that wouldn't die even with medicine.' That's a direct quote. She fought me on bringing Hartley because she didn't want to inconvenience us but I thought it might be nice to give her a break. Not that I mind hanging out with Hartley."

"I'm sorry about Jenna but I can assure you the kiddo isn't a big deal. Before I created the foundation and was more hands-on with nonprofits I spent a lot of time around kids." He laughed and hoped what he said next wouldn't be construed as weird. "I actually really love kids. I've always wanted a big family one day." Then without a thought left in his head he asked, "What about you? You want any kids?"

Desmond could have sworn it got so quiet in that house that you could hear a pin drop.

Riley's cheeks turned flame red just as Madi and his mother turned to stare at him behind her back.

Madi's eyes were as large as saucers. Her smile indicated she was damn near close to laughing.

Once again, Desmond was immensely grateful that his brothers weren't inside yet. First his lame *Wheel of Fortune* idea and now he was only upping his smooth game by asking if the woman he'd made out with that morning wanted a bunch of kids like he did.

And he'd pushed one heck of a spotlight on Riley to boot.

"What I *meant* to say was," he hurriedly tacked on, trying to salvage his foot-in-mouth moment, "do large families bother you? Because, if so, you're about to be really bothered."

The gods took pity on Desmond because, less than a second later, the front door flew open and in walked Caleb and his wife.

"Your favorite child is here, Ma," he yelled in greeting.

His wife, Nina, laughed behind him and pushed him into the house so Declan and she could get through.

Declan rolled his eyes.

"Being the loudest one doesn't a favorite child make," he pointed out.

Then Madi's mountain of a man brought up the rear, shutting the door behind him with a thoughtful look.

"Well, I'm the favorite son-in-law and I think that's pretty cool," he said.

"You've got that right," their mother piped in.

"You're her *only* son-in-law," Madi said. Their mother pushed past her and Desmond and Riley. She patted Julian's stomach.

"It's called son-in-love and he'll always be number one in my book."

"You're only feeding his ego, Ma," Madi said around a snort of laughter.

"Keep giving me grandbabies and I'll feed him whatever he wants," she responded.

That got everyone laughing. Even Riley. The blush from her cheeks had gone away.

"I don't mind this in the least."

THE FAMILY ONLY became more chaotic as they settled around the outdoor dining table on the back porch. The weather was still good enough that the chill was more pleasant than annoying. Riley sat between Desmond and Madi while Hartley floated between Riley's lap and his. Desmond was glad that Hartley seemed to have become taken with him.

Desmond wanted to spend more time with the boy's aunt and had a feeling that included him and Jenna.

A thought that surprised Desmond throughout the dinner.

It wasn't until Madi, Julian and Addison left and then his mother went inside to take a phone call that the conversation took a turn that led him away from any intriguing thoughts of the future.

"I have to say, Riley, I really am sorry about earlier," Declan dove in. His brow was creased and he looked every bit as sorry as Desmond had seen him.

"It's not your fault," she said.

"What's not your fault?" Desmond asked.

Declan shared a look with Riley.

What had he missed?

"I stopped by Mimi's Boutique on the way over here and Davies showed up." Desmond felt his blood pressure skyrocket. Riley touched the top of his hand. "He didn't do anything. Just said a few words and then left. He thought I was Jenna so he didn't stick around and bother me. I told Declan when I got here though, just so law enforcement knew he came back."

Desmond gave his older brother a look. Declan sighed.

"Jazz saw him leave but it wasn't like we were going to ask her to camp out there all day and night. He must've just driven back on in later when she was gone."

"He shouldn't be just coming back on in," Desmond said with heat in his words, even to his own ears.

"If he does it again I can take him in on harassment," he said to both of them. "If I grabbed him now his lawyer and that weird hair of hers would just do their dance again."

"Weird hair?" Riley asked.

Declan nodded.

"It was what I think is called platinum blond, but, good golly, it was so bright I could barely think when I first saw her."

"It's probably a distraction tactic," Caleb offered.

Declan shrugged.

"Whatever it is, it's attached to a woman who's very well connected and very *well funded* by the looks of the designer tags on everything she was wearing. I had to snap at a few of my deputies who were caught staring at her too long. You'd think they'd never seen a nice-looking lawyer the way they were gawking."

"Was she young?"

The question made sense but the tone in which Riley asked it didn't. Desmond faced her, knowing full well that the crinkle of concentration between his eyebrows that Madi always picked at him about was there.

Something was off with the siren sitting at his shoulder.

"Uh, yeah." Declan heard it too. His eyebrow rose high. "I'd say maybe midtwenties, which is why I assumed she was well connected, with how easily she got him out."

Every part of Riley had gone rigid.

Even Hartley sitting on her lap looked up at her face to try to puzzle out why the change had happened.

"What was the lawyer's name?"

Declan didn't have to think long.

"Maria Wendell."

Riley pushed her chair back but didn't stand. In turn all of the Nash men went on alert.

"Where is she?" Riley said. "That's what Davies kept asking."

Two large, dark and deeply worried eyes found Desmond's.

"What if Brett's attack wasn't just one of opportunity? What if he really did pick me on purpose? Or, really, Jenna," she continued. "She was supposed to be at the gala, not me. Geordi thought *I* was Jenna when we were at the park. And Davies has always been so bad at telling us apart, I just assumed since he saw Hartley he thought he was talking *to* Jenna today... But I think he actually knew who he was talking to."

Desmond's gut started yelling.

"He was asking where Jenna was," Desmond supplied.

Riley turned her gaze to Declan.

"The last time I saw Maria Wendell was at Macklin Tech right before I left the company," she continued. "Jenna and I have suspected since then that she was having an affair with Ryan."

Riley shook her head, a more palpable look passing over her expression.

Terror.

"The man in the suit at Second Wind called you Ms. Stone, not Riley," Declan added.

"Oh, God," Riley said in an almost whisper. She was back looking at Desmond.

His adrenaline shot up as she said the conclusion they had all just come to.

"What if everything that has happened to me hasn't been bad luck or some coincidence? What if it was all just really meant for Jenna?"

Chapter Fifteen

The Nash men took off so fast that Desmond could have believed they broke the sound barrier. He was hauling ass down Winding Road while Declan and Caleb made calls in the front and back seats.

Desmond used the time to focus on the road ahead of him, and not the growing sense of dread that had flipped in his stomach at Riley's last words to him. *Jenna's phone is going straight to voice mail. She never turns it off.*

Those had been the many, but absolutely effective, magic words.

Now they were about to have all of the sheriff's department on Willows Way.

But only after Desmond got them there first.

"We're the closest," Declan said after a few minutes. "There was a wreck out on County Road 11. It's got most of my people there right now."

"Jazz should get there but the way you're driving it'll definitely be after," Caleb added.

Then the inside of the truck became quiet.

They didn't speak again until the house came into view. A light was on inside the house.

"Let's go around the perimeter before we bust up in there," Caleb said, service weapon out. Declan followed suit. They exited the truck, careful to close the doors quietly, and fanned out. Caleb went around the house to the left. Declan went around the house to the right.

Desmond went straight to the front door.

He held his personal gun in one hand and unlocked the door with Riley's keys in the other.

He wasn't going to wait.

Not when Jenna might be in danger.

Jenna was about to be very scared or really thankful.

The house was mostly quiet. Something was making noise deeper within but he couldn't make out what it was. Desmond checked his gun again and took a deep breath. He'd never shot a person but wasn't above doing just that if necessary.

Because, in his gut, he knew Riley was right.

They'd spent too much time counting everything as coincidence and not enough of it stepping back to look at the entire picture. Not that Desmond could tell her exactly what the big picture was but now at least they were counting it as one series of events.

It wasn't just bad luck.

It was a design.

The sound of movement made Desmond stop in the doorway. He raised his gun, trying to place it.

He heard a *tink*. Something fell.

It was coming from the other side of the house, outside.

Desmond spun around, went back outside, and then to the corner. Much like he had with Riley at the law offices, he peeked around the side.

He could have sang in relief.

A mass of red curls could be seen just inside the opened window. The screen from it was on the grass.

Jenna was trying to go through the window.

Desmond slid his gun into the back of his pants and hurried over. Jenna, who was in the process of turning around so she could control the almost-six-foot drop thanks to a raised foundation, had one bare leg out and was working on her back-side.

She must have heard him. Her movements became frantic. She was trying to get back inside.

"Jenna," Desmond whispered, reaching out.

She tried to turn to see who it was but only lost her balance. With a strangled screech she slipped backward right out of the window. Desmond was glad he'd put his gun away as he caught the flailing woman like a child.

Her eyes were wide with terror. Even after she recognized him.

"Someone is in the house," she whispered. "I—I heard glass break."

Desmond set her down, angled her behind him and pulled his gun back out. He could see through the opened window that the light they'd seen from the road was in the hallway.

Jenna sucked in a breath as a shadow filled the doorway into the bedroom she'd just fallen out of.

"Move and I'll—"

A shot rang out before Desmond could offer up the threat.

Several things happened at once.

Jenna screamed. So loud and pure that Desmond couldn't help but think of Madi that day in the park. It sent fire into his veins.

He had to protect her.

But there was another heat happening. This one was physical and hurt like hell.

There was also a new sound. Two gunshots.

And it came from Desmond's gun.

The shadow in the doorway crumpled and groaned. The skewed vantage point of them being on the ground versus in the room sent the bullets into his leg.

Desmond readied to make a more critical hit if needed when yelling consumed the house.

Declan and Caleb converged on the man without an ounce of mercy. Desmond didn't lower his gun until he saw the other one kicked across the room.

"Are you okay?" he asked, spinning around to inspect Jenna. Even in the poor light she looked near fainting. "Jenna, *are you okay?*" he repeated. As if he'd physically shaken her awake she moved all at once.

"Am I okay? *Are you?*" she shrieked, hands reaching out to him. "Desmond, you've been shot!"

"What?" yelled Caleb from inside the house.

Declan started talking fast but it wasn't to them.

Desmond looked to where the heat had blossomed on his arm. There was a tear in his flannel at the arm. He *had* been shot after all.

"Well, look at that."

THE TEMPERATURE TURNED COLD like it was sensing their moods.

Riley was staring at the road that led to the main house with a ferocity that still felt as urgent as it had the moment she'd watched the Nash sons take off down it.

Now, even though she knew Jenna was alright, Riley couldn't loosen the worry that had put a vise over her heart. Because it wasn't just her twin she was worried about, it was also Desmond and his family. Every time she got to know them a little better she fell a little more in love with them. Their kindness, compassion and loyalty to one another were heartwarming.

Just what she and Jenna had needed after what happened in the world they'd left behind.

So when that blue Ford appeared on the road that split the ranch, Riley let out a ragged breath. When Jenna *and* Desmond were both inside, she nearly cried.

"Riley!"

"Jenna!"

In true Stone sister fashion they yelled for each other at the same time as Jenna got out. They embraced.

"I'm fine," Jenna assured her. "Desmond showed up just in time."

Riley pulled back to look her sister up and down. The pajama set she'd been wearing last time Riley had seen her had been replaced by pants and a hefty jacket. She also was shouldering a duffel bag. When she saw Riley look at it she gave a small smile of relief.

"Desmond insisted we stay with him tonight," she added. "I've decided we all are going to take him up on that offer. I packed you some clothes too."

Jenna's eyes roamed to the main house behind them. She was looking for her son.

"He's asleep in the living room," Riley said. "Dorothy read him a bedtime story that put him out flat."

Jenna grabbed and squeezed her hand in thanks and walked away.

Riley turned to seek out the second person

she'd been worried about. Desmond was slow getting out of his truck but he was smiling.

"I hope you don't mind bunking at my place ton—"

Riley didn't have long, long legs by any means but she somehow ate up the distance between them with surprising speed.

Desmond was warm as she pressed against him. Just like the kiss she gave him.

It was brief.

Riley stepped back and said the one thought on her mind. It was also brief.

"Thank you."

Desmond, bless him, didn't make a big deal about the kiss or the praise. He took his hat off.

"Yes, ma'am."

Headlights turned their attention to a truck coming up the road. The front door to the main house pushed open as Nina, Caleb's wife, ran to her husband when he got out. Riley felt a blush starting to burn in her cheeks as Nina did the same thing she had just done by pressing against Caleb and laying a big one on him.

When they parted Caleb caught their attention and nodded to the house.

Desmond sighed.

"Time to update everyone," he said.

HARTLEY DIDN'T MOVE an inch when the adults sat down and started talking in the living room but

Riley, Dorothy and Nina were all having a hard time not reacting in a big way to what they were hearing.

"Do you really think Geordi Green broke into the house to take Jenna?" Riley asked after they said Geordi had busted out the back window. "I know y'all don't like him but surely that's out of character for him."

A muscle in Desmond's jaw twitched.

Caleb handled the answer.

"This would definitely be an escalation for him, that's for sure. Writing garbage about us is one thing, breaking and entering and then—"

Desmond cleared his throat. Jenna tensed.

Caleb shook his head, seemingly changing what he had been about to say.

"Well, I just honestly don't know at this point what's going on with him, but considering what he said to you at the park, we have a direction we'll be going in first thing in the morning."

Riley raised her eyebrow and found her sister's gaze. If it was possible, Jenna tensed more.

"They think it could have something to do with Ryan, considering Davies and Maria have also shown up in town," Jenna said, dropping into a whisper. "I don't know why he would be after me now but out of everyone here I can say he probably hates me the most."

The question hung heavily in the air around

them. Riley took her sister's hand and kept it on top of the couch cushion.

"Regardless of whatever is going on and who's behind it, we'll get to the bottom of it," Caleb added. "As for Geordi, when he's out of surgery, Jazz will be on him faster than a horsefly on Ax's rump."

It was a colorful point. One that made Riley feel better.

"Until then I think it's high time everyone get some rest," Desmond said. Then to Riley and Jenna, "And until we understand what's going on, consider yourselves welcomed guests here on the Nash ranch."

Riley didn't like the situation they were in but she couldn't deny that Desmond's invitation made her feel better.

THE NEXT HALF HOUR was spent saying goodbye to one another—even though no one in the house was actually leaving the ranch grounds—and transitioning to Desmond's home. Dorothy insisted it was fine if the girls wanted to stay with her but Riley already knew where she wanted to be.

And, by this point, everyone seemed to understand that the Stone sisters were a package deal, including one extremely sleepy Hartley.

Desmond carried the little man with one arm

protectively wrapped around him. The sight reminded her of their earlier conversation.

Did she want a lot of kids?

Riley smiled into the night air.

She hadn't been about to admit to anyone at dinner that, yes, a big family had always been a goal in her life. She'd just never found the right time to start reaching for that goal with Davies. Though, again, maybe that had been her heart's way of warning her about the man.

But now? Following behind the strapping, messy-haired, drool-worthy cowboy holding one of the few people she loved with her entire being?

Riley found herself wondering what his dark hair and her curls would look like on a child.

"Does he have abs?"

Riley spun her head around so fast it was like she was in *The Exorcist.*

"Come again?"

Jenna kept on like they were talking about the weather.

"I asked if he had abs," she repeated, motioning to Desmond. "He literally caught me in his arms after I fell out of Hartley's bedroom window and it was like hitting a wall. You said you didn't *you know* with him but you did see him shirtless, right?"

Normally, Riley would have swatted away—physically and verbally—the question, but there was an undercurrent to Jenna's words. A small waver that she doubted anyone else would recognize.

Jenna was scared.

And rightly so.

Being attacked at her home was one thing, but the idea that Ryan could be connected to it?

Riley didn't blame her for the fear. Heck, she was feeling it too.

"Remember when we first watched *Magic Mike* and you said that no man really has a body that yummy? That they're probably all computer generated?" Riley whispered instead. Jenna's eyes widened. A whisper of a smile crossed her lips.

"Really? *That* nice?"

Riley nodded, matter-of-factly.

"Abs. For. Days."

Desmond looked over his shoulder as they both devolved into giggles. Bless him again, he didn't ask.

RILEY, JENNA AND HARTLEY opted to stay in the same guest bedroom upstairs. It was down the hall from Desmond's, as was another empty room where Madi had lived before starting the bed-and-breakfast. Still the women hadn't accepted the offer for each of them to have their own room.

Just as Desmond didn't admit that ever since that kiss out by his truck, he'd been thinking about Riley staying in his.

Instead he gave them privacy and showered in

his en suite while they used the hall bathroom to get ready for bed. Before saying good-night he promised to keep them updated as soon as he had any information.

Desmond also wanted to make sure he had his own privacy as he undressed and got into the shower. Sure, a certain part of him was really craving some company but his more level-headed side had reminded himself that he didn't want Riley to know he'd been shot. Just as they had all agreed, even Jenna, at the Stone house, that they would keep that information away from their mother.

He knew it didn't make sense to ask that of Riley's twin—and, honestly, he knew Riley could handle the news—but Desmond couldn't shake the look of worry that had stared back at him at dinner.

He didn't want Riley to go through that needlessly, if he could help it.

Not saying that he believed she would react the same as his mother, but still, Desmond was glad he was able to shower and clean the blood he'd hidden with his jacket.

When he was done, he toweled dry, brushed his teeth and slipped on a pair of boxers. He was contemplating putting a shirt on over his wound, worried about getting blood on his sheets, when a knock sounded on the door.

"Just a sec," he called, trying to spot his robe.

It was across the room. He didn't have a chance to traverse the space before the bedroom door opened wide.

Riley Stone, in an oversize T-shirt that cut off at the middle of her thighs and had a picture of French fries on it, stared back at him with anger clear in her eyes.

Desmond realized then that leaving her out of the loop had been a bad, bad idea.

"You were *shot*?"

Chapter Sixteen

Riley said it in a low volume but it came out strong. Then she shut the door behind her and Desmond knew he was really in trouble now.

"Listen, it was only a graze," he tried, putting both his hands up in surrender. The movement made the gash across his bicep hurt. He winced. "I didn't want to go worrying anyone over something that wasn't a big deal."

Riley walked up to him, hands still on her hips.

"Over something that wasn't a big deal? Jenna said not only did you take a bullet that could have been for her, but you also *shot Geordi twice*." She waved her hands around, as if confused as to what thought she wanted to grab on to first. "*All* of those things are big deals. Ones you didn't tell me!"

Desmond lowered his hands and sighed.

"You've been through a lot, is all. I didn't want to add anything unless I had to."

Riley's expression softened. Then her eyes

traveled to the gash on his arm. There was a bandage over it but still her look of concern grew.

"That's what I wanted to avoid," he added. "That look."

She snorted.

"I think if someone gets shot, it calls for *some* worry." She lightly touched his arm. "Does it hurt a lot?"

Desmond tried to control his breathing.

And the rest of his body.

Riley's touch was innocent, he knew that, but the desire it stirred within him wasn't.

"Not enough to bother me."

Even to his ears his words came out differently than they had before. It caught Riley's attention. She glanced down at his bare chest and then immediately took a step back. Her cheeks became flushed.

"Wow. I just burst in here, didn't I?" she said around nervous laughter. "I'm so sorry. Jenna just finally told me what happened and I was going to wait for morning to tell you off—not that I was really going to tell you off or anything—but then I couldn't shake it and—"

Desmond crashed his lips into hers. Her words died between their lips. It pushed him closer to the point of no return. He made sure to disengage momentarily from their lip-lock to say something before the start of their next adventure.

"Every time we've kissed you've either been

apologizing or thanking me," he said, gravel in his words. "I'm here to tell you now, you don't owe me a thing. You don't have to say sorry or tiptoe around me and what you want. Got it?"

Riley nodded. Her lips were already rosy.

He smirked as he continued.

"But, I'm here to tell you right now what I want and if that lines up with something you're interested in, you let me know." He brought his hand up and ran it across her cheek. Then he looked at her lips and knew the woman in front of him, with wild, wild hair and wearing a shirt with fries on it, had the power to make him do whatever she wanted without question.

"Riley Stone, I'd really like to show you a damn good time. Right now. Here in my bed."

For a second, Desmond thought she might turn him down but then Riley did what she did best.

She pressed her lips against his with purpose.

Desmond supposed that was her way of saying she liked that idea too.

RILEY'S NIGHTSHIRT WAS THROWN so far away she wouldn't be surprised if later she found it in another state.

Desmond's lips moved to her neck and then slid their way right down to her breast. Riley moaned in response.

It encouraged the man.

When he dropped to his knees and slid her sleep shorts off, Riley nearly wept.

But Desmond wasn't quite so direct.

He let out a primal sort of growl and was back to his feet in a flash. Then he gently threw Riley on the bed.

It took all she could muster not to yell, "Take me!"

Instead she watched with bated breath as the man she often called cowboy crawled across the bed and right on top of her.

Unlike their time on the living-room floor there was no awkward innocence or tentative prompting.

Desmond had made it clear he wanted her.

And she wanted to return the favor.

Riley wrapped her legs around his waist and pushed up against his lips like he was the last drink of water in the desert. It surprised the cowboy but in the best way. He reacted by deepening their kiss and using one arm to keep her against him.

Then he flipped them both.

Riley let out a small laugh in surprise. Desmond broke their kiss, eyes hooded and lips swollen. Riley was afraid she'd offended him with the noise but then those same lips pulled up at the corners.

That smile.

That Desmond Nash smile.

It was one in a million.

And more than worked its magic.

Riley relieved Desmond of his boxers while the last vestige of her clothes disappeared too.

When he pushed inside, Riley let him know just how much she enjoyed it. He, in turn, wasn't leaving her wondering. The comforter and sheets twisted. Moans of ecstasy escaped. A rhythm was created, kept and then sped along to a wonderful conclusion.

What had started as a chance meeting at a party had become something so much more, and as Riley lay naked in his arms, breathless and slick with sweat, she couldn't help but feel the shift in her future.

Overlook had been a way station.

A pit stop.

A respite.

A transition that she'd intended to end after she'd made sure Jenna was okay.

Plans for her career, her future family and her happiness weren't ready to be made. Not here. Not in Overlook.

Yet, listening to the still-racing heartbeat of Desmond Nash, Riley found that she was dangerously close to including the cowboy in all of them.

THEY LAY TOGETHER. They laughed together. They showered together. They lay back down together. And they fell asleep together.

It was a lot closer than he'd expected to become with someone in a while.

However, when Desmond woke and found Riley was still there next to him, he was happy it was with her.

A siren who hadn't led him astray.

The lamp on the nightstand bathed the bedroom in low light. It illuminated the relaxed face of the woman at his side. Even though she'd used his body wash, he still could smell the lavender on her. It had a calming effect on him, he realized.

Desmond shifted onto his back. Despite having just woken up he was still dead tired. He hadn't been sleeping that great lately. Not since the night of the gala, if he was being honest with himself.

Not since he'd seen the graffiti at Second Wind's construction site.

If Ryan Alcaster *was* trying to get to Jenna or *get* Jenna, how did the construction site fit into any of it?

Was it a distraction or a pointed jab to ruffle his feathers?

And how did Brett Calder and, possibly, the Fixers fit into any of it?

Desmond closed his eyes again, feeling his body tense in frustration. Madi had once worried about the family's bad luck. Their constant falling in with trouble was pretty damning when it came to the accusation.

But without trouble you wouldn't have gotten to know her, Desmond thought a split second later. *There'd be no Riley in your bed.*

That would be one heck of a shame, if he did say so himself.

Desmond decided to wake up early, make the Stones some breakfast and then dive into a giant cup of coffee and figure out *something* that was going on so they could find some peace. He started to roll over to turn off the lamp when two things happened on top of each other.

A board in the kitchen floor, right under his room, the one Madi used to complain about, yelled out its horrible whine.

And then Desmond realized he hadn't just woken up, he'd *been* woken up.

Instead of turning the lamp off he went for his phone. There were no new messages or calls. After everything the Nashes had been through in the last few years everyone knew not to just creep around without some kind of warning. Which was why his mother had rung the doorbell the other day and not burst right on in.

The clock on his phone read 4:05 a.m. Nashes were also early risers, came with the territory of helping run a ranch growing up, but that was a little too early for normal.

Surely no one had broken in, he hoped.

Brett was dead, Geordi was in the hospital, but Davies?

Desmond got out of bed in a flash. Riley stirred as he went for his jeans and put them on in record time. He cursed beneath his breath when he realized his gun was still at the department. He had another in the safe but it was downstairs in his office.

"Desmond?"

Riley was sitting up and blinking away sleep. Then her eyes were wide. She'd noticed his worry.

"I think someone is downstairs," he whispered. "Could be nothing, could be something."

Riley vaulted out of bed, impressing Desmond with how quiet the movement was, and started for the door. The fun fries shirt contrasted with her serious expression.

"I have to make sure Jenna and Hartley are okay," she explained, low.

Desmond caught her hand before she could hit the doorknob. For a moment he saw anger flash through her. He understood it just as quick.

No one could stand between him and his family.

Just like no one could stand between her and her sister and nephew.

So Desmond wasn't even going to try.

"Let me go out first. If I don't yell up to you as soon as I go down the stairs, call Caleb. His house is down the road." He tucked his phone in her hand. "Don't come downstairs."

He held her gaze until she nodded.

Then he kissed her, opened the door, and they went their separate ways. Riley to the guest bedroom down the hall and Desmond to the stairs. He made a fist, angry he hadn't thought to keep a weapon in his room, and descended.

Since there were people staying in his house who weren't familiar with it, Desmond had left a light on over the sink in the kitchen and a lamp on in the living room. It didn't do much for the small hallway between or the rest of the first floor but it was enough to see that his family wasn't in his house.

But someone else definitely was.

Desmond pushed back up against the wall next to the bottom step of the stairs. Around the corner from him was someone he didn't recognize.

But given the shock of platinum-blond hair, Desmond assumed it was the fancy lawyer he'd heard about from his brothers.

Maria Wendell.

In his living room at four in the morning.

Desmond took a quick breath and crouched. He eased his head around the corner again.

She was looking toward the front door, as if her being there was normal. She even had her fingers threaded together and against her stomach.

The odd stance showcased the lack of weapon in them.

Something wasn't right.

Why was she there?

Movement across from him in the kitchen changed everything. Desmond didn't even have the chance to move.

A man walked out into the hallway, gun raised. He was wearing a three-piece suit.

"If you lunge at me, I'll still be able to get at least one shot off," he said, voice cool and calm. "Considering how close we are, that shot will probably cripple, if not kill, you. Then how will you help Ms. Stone?" He nodded toward the living room. "Let's go in there."

Desmond swore but followed directions. Making noise to wake him had been on purpose. Just as Maria had been a distraction.

The blonde didn't look at all surprised as Desmond stopped in front of her. He angled his body so he could see them both.

"I can't believe that worked," Maria said to the man in the suit. She looked Desmond up and down. "And you were right, no gun."

The man shrugged.

"He gave it to his brother after he shot Geordi and his safe is downstairs."

"Who are you?" Desmond bit at him.

The man ignored him. He kept the gun steady and addressed Maria.

"One of them is probably calling the Nash who lives the closest. You have less than a minute to get her. I suggest you go do that now."

Maria pulled a small pistol from the pocket of her coat.

"*Fine.* Just make sure he doesn't touch me or I *will* shoot him. *Comprende?*"

The man in the suit adopted a look of quick anger.

"You kill him, or anyone in this house, and I will be the only, and the last, problem you ever have. *Comprende?*"

Desmond didn't understand the directive but Maria's gusto was doused by it.

"What do you even want with her?" Desmond asked, trying to stall.

Maria snorted.

"You think just asking me a question is going to get me talking?" She glanced at the man in the suit. "If I can't kill you then I'm certainly not going to talk to you."

Desmond didn't hate the fact that he was about to ruin her day. The moment she was next to him Desmond threw his shoulder into her as hard as he could, two guns in the room be damned.

He expected a gunshot to go off but the only sound that followed the hit was Maria's short-lived screech as her legs smacked the coffee table and she flailed over. The pistol hit the wood first and then slid as the table toppled with her weight.

Desmond lurched for the weapon but the man in the suit surprised him with a swift kick to the side. It was Desmond who stumbled now. He caught his balance before falling all the way to the floor and then spun on his heel.

Only to be staring into the barrel of a gun.

Maria was cussing up a storm but the man in the suit was still as unruffled as they came.

He looked Desmond right in the eye when he spoke.

"She's not allowed to kill her. Not yet."

Desmond tried to avoid the knockout hit but the man in the suit was too fast. The world turned black before he even landed on the floor.

DESMOND STARED UP at the ceiling and saw white shiplap.

His house.

Living room.

Pain.

It weighed down his body, his head, while at the same time burning him.

Fragments of memories remained scattered around him, even when the yelling started.

"Desmond?"

Caleb's face, full of worry, and his gun both came into view. He ran to Desmond and crouched in front of him.

"God, that's so much blood," he said, touching a spot on Desmond's head that made him suck in a breath. "What happened?"

The question was magnetized. It brought those

scattered fragments of memories together and formed one terrifying reality.

Desmond pushed up, stumbled to the side as his head spun at the movement, but kept moving forward.

"Maria and the man in the suit came for Jenna," he hurried. "He knocked me out."

Desmond hated the words.

Hated them almost as much as he hated the man who had done it.

"Riley? Jenna?" he yelled around the hatred flowing through him. He took the stairs two at a time. Caleb was on his heels and had his hand on his back.

No one answered his call. But that didn't stop Desmond from yelling out. He continued to do it all the way into the guest bedroom. Even at the sight of an empty room, he still called out for them.

For her.

"Desmond!"

A woman's voice floated from somewhere else in the house.

"My room," he realized, turning.

Together they rushed into the bedroom and were met with a weird sight.

"Was your dresser in front of the closet before?" Caleb asked after flipping the light on. The dresser had always stood next to the door, not in front of it.

Desmond shook his head.

"No, it wasn't."

Someone started banging against the closet door it was covering. Wordlessly Caleb pushed it out of the way. The second the door was clear, Desmond flung it open.

A sea of wild red curls encased a tear-stained face. Dark eyes rimmed with water looked back at him. The fun shirt with fries on the front contrasted with her look of anguish.

"Oh, Desmond," she said, voice breaking. "She made me."

Movement at the back of the closet showed a scared Hartley. He hurried up to them and grabbed his mom's hand.

Desmond turned to his brother and hated what he said more than anything else in the world.

"They took Riley."

Chapter Seventeen

Hours went by.

Hours.

Desmond absolutely felt them.

So had every Nash alive. Not only had Maria and the man in the suit taken Riley, they'd done so from their home. No one had seen them come onto the ranch and no one had seen them leave. Not even Caleb who had jumped in his truck and hightailed it over after Riley had called.

Riley.

Desmond knew it was useless to try to move his thoughts away from how worried he was. How angry he felt. How helpless he'd become since.

She heard them talking and said we needed to hide, Jenna had tearfully explained. *Then she—she said if it was Ryan that we—we needed to change because he knew about that stupid fries shirt. I told her no but then she pointed to Hartley and I—I did it. I switched clothes.* She'd held Hartley tight to her chest and barely was able to

keep from all out sobbing. *Then— Then she told
me to be quiet for Hartley and—and she pushed
me and shut the door. I couldn't open it. Then I
heard you.*

Desmond didn't know Jenna as well as he
knew her sister but he had put his arms around
her and Hartley, hoping to help her somehow.

We're going to get her back, he had promised.
We're going to get her back.

Now, hours later, Desmond was at the sheriff's department, waiting for their only lead to
pan out. Judging by Caleb's expression after he
came out of the interrogation room, panning out
wasn't happening.

"Davies is barking for a lawyer again," he
greeted.

"A lawyer? You mean the same one who *took
Riley*?" Desmond put his hands on his hips.
"Please, then, by all means let him get her out
here."

They both knew that wasn't going to happen.

Maria Wendell had disappeared completely.
Last Desmond heard no one even knew where
she had been for at least two weeks.

Ryan Alcaster included.

Declan was in Kilwin talking to him and *his*
lawyer. So far that had yielded zero results.

Which left them with Evan Davies. He'd been
staying in a hotel outside of Kilwin. Declan had

pulled some strings and gotten him sent to the department.

A lot of good that was doing them now.

"I don't think he's lying about not knowing about what happened tonight," Caleb said after a moment. "He seemed genuinely surprised."

"But he does know *something* and he's too much of a coward to say anything."

Caleb nodded in agreement.

"From what we know of him he seems to only have a backbone in the corporate world. Out here, in real life, he looks like he's afraid of his own shadow. Or Ryan Alcaster's or the man in the suit's. Whoever is pulling the strings because you know it's not him."

Desmond grunted his displeasure.

"I've met men like him before. I vowed Second Wind would never employ anyone like that." Desmond ran a hand along his chin. There was already stubble there. He paused as a thought occurred to him. He lowered his voice. "I've met men like him before. I know how he thinks."

Caleb's eyebrow rose in question. It fell just as fast as he figured out the answer.

"You want to talk to him," he spelled out.

"I want to find Riley, and if Davies won't talk to law enforcement, maybe he'll talk to a CEO."

CALEB SHUT THE DOOR behind him. He was going to keep watch because he was a good brother, but mostly, because he knew Riley meant something different to Desmond.

Even without saying anything, it was simply understood.

And they were running out of time to save her.

Now they were breaking the rules and Desmond wasn't going to leave that room until he got the answers he wanted.

"I don't know anything," Davies said, sitting up straight. "And I'm not going to talk to any of you until I have a lawyer in front of me."

Desmond knew two things going into the interrogation room. For one, he knew he looked like a good ol' country boy. Jeans, flannel, boots and his Stetson. He knew those jeans were worn, the flannel was rumpled, his boots had dried mud on them and his cowboy hat sometimes gave outsiders the impression that, for some reason, he wasn't as smart as them.

What he also knew, and what Davies was about to find out, was that Desmond wasn't leaving that room until he had a way to find Riley.

So, he removed his cowboy hat, set it down on the metal table between them and took the seat his brother had been sitting in minutes before.

Davies eyed him with defiance.

That defiance wasn't going to fly with Desmond.

"I'm going to go ahead and stop you right there," Desmond began, threading his hands together on the tabletop. He made sure to keep his voice even. "I'm not law enforcement, never have been. Which means, legally, I don't have to provide you with anything. Least of all a lawyer. So singing that I-want-a-lawyer song isn't going to make me do anything other than get really annoyed."

"If you're not law enforcement you're not supposed to be in here," Davies tried. There was more bite in his voice than Desmond liked. He waved his hand to dismiss the thought.

"Listen, I get it—you want to be alone right now and I respect that. I surely wouldn't want to be in here either." Desmond motioned to the room around them. "These walls? Once you're inside them they mean something different to everyone you meet." He leaned back a touch in his chair, careful to keep his body language light and easy. "Some will think it's exciting you were in here, some even sexy, but others? They'll think you did something wrong. Something bad. Worst of all? Two times in less than forty-eight hours makes you look guilty as sin."

"I didn't *do* anything," Davies said, voice raised.

Desmond shrugged.

"Exactly. You didn't do *anything*. When you were asked what you knew about Ryan Alcaster's, Maria Wendell's and the man in the suit's involvement in the attack and abduction of your ex-wife, you didn't say or do *anything.*" Desmond cocked his head to the side and pointed at the man opposite him. "And *that* is what everyone is going to know at the end of this."

Davies was unable to hide his flinch. Desmond guessed the man already had gone over that thought in his head.

And he hadn't liked it.

Desmond leaned forward. He knew he could break the man and he was ready to bring it home.

"Do you know that my dad was a detective?" he started. "A really *good* one too. When my siblings and I were younger we were so intrigued about all aspects of his job. But, for me, I was mostly curious about how he was able to make these people who had found themselves in such unflattering positions talk. How he could, as a highly respected and well-known law-enforcement person, get these hardened criminals to tell him what he needed to know. So, one day I asked him."

Desmond readjusted his casual lean so that he was sitting up tall.

"What he told me really stuck with me. He said, *You know, Des, every person on this green earth wants to talk, to tell their story. It's in our nature. And, just like everyone wants to talk, everyone has at least the one person they want to talk to. The only challenge is becoming that one person.*" He once again motioned to the room around them. "And this is where he did it. Day in and day out, case after case, he became someone the other person needed before they said a word."

Desmond thumbed back to the door that led to the hallway.

"My brothers, that detective and the sheriff, they took my father's job and the lessons that went along with it and became the law themselves. But me? When I realized I could help people just by talking? Well, I turned that lesson into a smile." To put emphasis on his point he brought up the corners of his lips with ease. "I became known as the charming one because I figured out the secret. From investors, volunteers and potential donors to boardroom meetings and legal teams to my mother's book club, they all wanted the same thing those hardened criminals and wrongly accused wanted. To talk. All I had to do was become a good listener."

Desmond dropped his sweet act. He leaned in again, his elbows on the table.

"So I could sit here as long as they're allowed to hold you and go through the motions all in the hope you'd finally tell yours." He jabbed one of his index fingers down on the tabletop. Davies was staring at him, unable to look away.

Good.

"Or you can finally do the right thing and just tell me what you know. If you ever loved Riley at all, you owe her that."

A silence settled between them. Davies didn't blink. The heat kicked on somewhere else in the building. Shoes scuffed against tile floor nearby.

Then, all at once, Evan Davies let out a sigh of defeat, his entire body dragging down. There was a hunch to his shoulders when he finally spoke.

"I honest to God don't know where she is and I don't know how Maria Wendell or the man in the suit are involved. I also don't know if Ryan Alcaster is really behind any of it…"

"But?"

Davies let out another long, disheartened breath.

"But I do know the motive, if he is."

"And that is?" Desmond was on the edge of his seat. The door opened. Caleb came in and shut it behind him.

Apparently he had been in the viewing room.

Davies looked between them, but thankfully, didn't have to be talked into continuing to say what he was about to say.

He was just as defeated as he answered.

"Ryan didn't actually get all his money and success by building from the ground up. When he joined Macklin Tech he already was living off his father's money. *Sam* Alcaster inherited a fortune from his uncle when he realized he himself wouldn't have kids. Sam was extremely proud that he could pass that wealth, plus the money he'd added to it over the course of his life, to his son. That had always been the plan." Davies looked uncomfortable. He shifted in his seat. "A few weeks after the divorce, Ryan showed up in the Atlanta office visibly upset. Maria was in-house and saw it too. We were his friends so we followed him into a conference room to see what was wrong. He shut the door and locked it. I should have known right then that he was trouble."

"You should have known it after you found out he was beating his wife."

Desmond didn't mean for the jab to slip out— not that he regretted it, they just didn't have the time for it—and Davies flinched.

"What was wrong with him?" Caleb interjected, keeping the new information moving.

"Apparently his father had done some digging into the divorce," Davies continued. "He didn't understand why Jenna was given full custody and cut every part of her life with Ryan off."

"Let me guess," Desmond jumped in. "He found out what his son had been doing."

Davies nodded.

"He had hired a private investigator. One who found records, video and pictures of when Jenna was hospitalized. He put it together after that and then he changed his will."

Money. It was about money.

Desmond should have known.

"Ryan isn't getting a penny?"

Davies shook his head.

"Sam is leaving every cent of his fortune to Hartley... Which can only be accessed and used by Hartley's legal guardian if he receives it before the age of twenty-two."

For a moment no one spoke.

Desmond shared a look with his brother. Neither liked what they had just heard.

"So Ryan wants custody of Hartley to secure his original inheritance," Caleb said.

"But the only reason Jenna didn't expose Ryan in the first place was because she'd been given full custody of Hartley without a fight," Desmond recapped. "There's no way she would have been quiet if he'd tried to get full custody again. She'd out him and everything he'd done."

A sickening thought blossomed in Desmond's head. He saw it reflected in Davies's expression.

"Unless something happened to Jenna," he realized. "Brett Calder, the Fixer. Geordi and Maria. He's not getting his hands dirty, he's dirtying everyone else's."

"He never said he was going to do anything but he very clearly realized the only way to get his inheritance was through Hartley," Davies said. "I assumed he was spending so much time with Maria because she was helping him, I don't know, build a case or something. But then I heard about a news story of famous small-town triplets saving a twin just outside of Kilwin. When I saw that it was Riley and that Jenna was also in town, I worried Ryan had come up with a more malicious plan."

Desmond was getting hot.

Angry.

"Why didn't you warn her then? Why not warn law enforcement? Why were you at the construction site instead?"

"Because of me," Davies said, confusing both Nashes. He blew out a frustrated breath and explained. "I didn't say anything to anyone about Ryan beating his wife. I sacrificed my marriage to keep that secret, all because I believed my job was that important." Davies looked to Desmond. "You said it yourself in so many words—being charming can be a tool but it can also be a weapon. Do you know how many friends Ryan has? How many 'me's he's mentored and helped through the years? He's not a man you take on head-to-head. You have to catch him in the act. So I tried to." Another long sigh. He was so hunched over by now that Desmond had to angle his gaze down. "I said I found a way to get him what he wanted and asked him to meet me at a place where we could make that happen. I chose the construction site because of how much the media around here seems to love you Nashes. I figured the response time would be quicker and the coverage greater if anything went south with me trying to record his confession without him realizing it. But when I got there I was met by the man in the suit. He said he had been sent there to talk to me. He never specifically said Ryan, but, well, I guess that's the only person who knew I was going there."

"Then Marty showed up."

Davies shook his head with vigor, sitting up a little taller than before.

"I never saw Marty. He must have been on the third floor already. I swear," he hurried. "When I heard you downstairs I panicked and ran."

"And the next day Maria Wendell was your lawyer," Caleb said, disgust clear in his tone.

"You have to understand, Maria has been a friend for the last several months. Calling her didn't seem that crazy at the time." He shook his head. "I didn't know she was involved in Ryan's plans."

Desmond rubbed his chin again. In the late hours of the night Riley had done the same motion and laughed.

The memory made him feel warm and hollowed out at the same time.

He fixed Davies with a stare he hoped hurt.

"You know Ryan, better than anyone we've talked to," he said. "And now you're going to tell *us* everything."

Desmond didn't ask if he understood.

Because, *not* understanding wasn't an option.

Desmond had to find her.

There was no other option.

Chapter Eighteen

The AC unit made a tired, wheezing sound as the heat cut on.

It reminded Riley of a prop plane that had been flying without any problems, only to lose its engine while at a cruising altitude. Then, by some miracle, the propeller would kick back into gear.

The unit beneath the window would strain, sputter and then stop altogether. When Riley believed it had finally died—finally giving in to its inevitable mechanical death—it would cut on with some *clank*s and then slide into the wheeze. Where it would keep that pace for at least half an hour before doing the entire loud dance all over again.

It was driving Riley insane.

Along with rope that had been thoroughly wrapped around her and the chair she was sitting on. Maria might have been slight in frame and have supermodel good looks but Riley had spent the last several hours seeing the demon beneath the makeup and expensive clothes. Not to mention a surprising proficiency at tying knots. Ones that didn't come undone no matter how much you moved.

Maria let out a loud huff just as the AC chugged back to life again. Riley didn't bother turning to look over her shoulder at the woman. She was used to her routine too by now. The blonde was sitting on one of the two beds with her heels kicked off and a cell phone in front of her face.

And apparently not getting the call that she wanted.

This time Maria's sigh was punctuated by noise that fell somewhere between a grunt and a scream. It wasn't loud enough to escape the hotel-room walls but it did make Riley's muscles tense in anticipation.

She'd had every intention in the world, when she switched with Jenna, to try to get Maria and the man in the suit as far away from the ranch as possible and, only then, to try to fight her way out. She'd heard Desmond, Maria and the man in the suit talking in the living room at his house.

For whatever reason, Maria wasn't allowed to kill any of them.

But Riley wasn't betting on that verbal agreement to hold. She had gotten into the car with them and immediately started to make a game plan for when they stopped again.

Yet, the moment they'd pulled up to a roadside motel on the outskirts of Kilwin, the man in the suit had turned in his seat to face her. He had said something that made Riley's stomach go cold.

Good luck.

Those two words had taken away Riley's hope of escaping. When he left the car right after and then Maria swung around with her pistol aimed, that hope further deteriorated.

I've made a career out of getting results, she had said. *So here are the results I'm going to see and incur based on what you do now.* The motel was a long two-story building that was shaped like a warped *L.* She motioned toward the office. A woman and a preteen were sitting at a white iron patio table next to the door. A book was open in front of the girl and the woman seemed to be enjoying a mug of something. *That woman there is Abela. She's the day manager and a single mother to Dina, sitting across from her. They know and like me so I could walk right up to them and shoot Abela in the face before either would think to be worried.*

Riley had gasped. Maria had held up her other hand to silence her.

Or you could come quietly into my room where we'll sit and wait for me to get a call.

Riley had glanced from Abela and Dina to the busy road they'd just come off. Maria hadn't missed it.

Listen. Don't underestimate me just because I'm not wearing a suit, she said with a snap of her fingers. *If you say anything or if you run, I won't try to shut you up and I won't try to chase you.* She'd pointed back at the mom and daughter. *I* will *walk across the parking lot and shoot Abela in the face right in front of her daughter.*

You're disgusting, Riley had seethed.

Maria had smiled.

I'm a woman of my word and I've given you two options and the results of picking either. Now, once I put this gun in my pocket, will you follow me calmly to my room or are you ready to be the reason a sweet girl is about to become an orphan?

Riley had seen it then. The intention. The promise.

She had believed Maria.

So she'd abandoned her plans of escape.

Let's go.

Now hours had gone by, and that call Maria had been waiting for still hadn't come. As for conversation while they had waited? Riley would have had better luck with the old AC unit.

Not having a talk with Maria wasn't breaking Riley's heart, though. The blonde hadn't just proven to be malicious; she was also impatient. Riley didn't want to exacerbate her nasty tendencies by digging into that impatience.

Plus, Riley wanted to give Desmond as much time as possible to find her.

Because Riley knew he would try his damnedest.

"What is *taking* so long?"

Maria kicked her feet against the bed like she was Hartley after being denied fruit gummy snacks. Riley looked over her shoulder, unable to hide her growing annoyance with the woman.

"Don't look at me like that," Maria snapped, stilling herself.

"Like what?" Riley couldn't help but say. "Like I'm tied to a chair, being held captive and not happy about it? Are you saying I should smile instead?"

Maria was fast. She was off the bed and standing in front of Riley wearing a pair of very expensive shoes.

"Don't look at me like you don't know why you're in this situation in the first place." She bent over, hands on the arms of the chair. Riley refused to flinch. "If you hadn't lied in the first place, this never would have happened. You did this. Not him."

Up until then Riley had been working under the assumption that Ryan was behind everything. It was the best theory that she had, but one that wasn't proven on account of Maria's lack of communication. Now there was no room left to interpret another mastermind.

"Ryan."

"A man who deserved, and got, way better than you." Maria was smirking. Riley hated the sight.

"A man who beats his wife deserves to rot in jail," she bit out.

The slap against her cheek happened so fast that Riley didn't have time to react. Pain radiated across the side of her face. Maria's composure had cracked again, the malicious side of her personality pushing through with growing aggression.

"That man did everything for you, and how did you repay him? Lie at every turn," she said. "We both know he didn't lay a hand on you."

"I was hospitalized," Riley exclaimed, keeping in line with the lie that she was her sister. "I have pictures and witnesses!"

"Having a sister lie to corroborate your story doesn't equal any evidence. It just means she's a filthy liar like you are."

Riley could feel the heat of anger burning through her. Ryan was still tainting every part of their lives.

"It wasn't a lie, but I'm assuming, you'll find that out at some point." Riley lowered her voice. "He was nice in the beginning with me too."

The second slap Riley *did* see coming. She was able to brace before Maria's hand connected with the already-stinging cheek. Still, Riley continued. She was finally getting somewhere with the woman.

"I'm going to go out on a limb here and take that as a confirmation that you're with Ryan now.

But, if you're so happy and sure of him being a good man, then why am I here? Why have you been after me?"

Maria took a step back, standing to her full height, and pulled her arms over her chest. She'd ditched her laughable trench coat on the bed and was sporting an expensive blouse-and-pencil-skirt set. Not that Riley ever wanted to attack or kidnap someone but she had to believe if she did, she would wear something a little less corporate while doing it.

"Because even though your lies didn't fool everyone, they did get to Sam. But once that's cleared up we can finally get on with our lives again."

Riley's eyebrow shot up despite trying to remain impassive. Sam Alcaster? Hartley's grandfather? From what Riley knew from Jenna, Sam had genuinely seemed to be a good, caring man. He'd even called the house to talk to Hartley on the phone from time to time, even when Hartley was too young to make any sense.

Then again, Ryan had seemed to be a genuinely nice man too at one point.

"What do you mean, once it's cleared up?" Riley asked. "Whatever you do to me won't take away from the fact that the authorities know who you are by now. They know you took me. The only chance you have at getting on with the rest of your life will be if you let me go and turn yourself in."

Maria was unfazed.

In fact, she smiled.

"You couldn't even begin to guess at my future."

The bed started to vibrate. Both women looked at Maria's phone dancing on the comforter.

Riley couldn't see the caller ID but when Maria scooped it up, she smiled wide.

Ryan.

"Hey, babe." She answered the phone with hearts in her eyes and sex in her voice. There was no question in Riley's mind that Ryan had absolutely hooked Maria.

And that it would spell the end for the woman.

Maybe sooner rather than later too. Maria's face fell two seconds into the conversation. She turned and headed to the bathroom.

"It's not my… But I had to… But I…"

Riley strained to hear more but Maria shut the bathroom door.

The urge to try to escape pulsed through her veins like blood. If Maria didn't have the pistol on her, she would have tried. All Riley could think about now, though, was the mother-daughter pair living their lives a few rooms down from them.

Again, Riley believed Maria would absolutely take out her anger at Riley escaping on them.

She wasn't willing to risk that.

For a phone call Maria had waited hours to receive, it was surprisingly brief. Only a minute or two went by before she huffed out of the bathroom with an expression that said she was close to throwing another tantrum.

"Not what you wanted to hear?" Riley asked, readying to apply pressure to the idea that Ryan was *not* a good man again. "I told you. Ryan has a short fuse. He—"

"He's waiting for us," Maria interrupted. Riley had misread that look of anger the woman had been wearing. She simply seemed annoyed now at the prospect of doing more work.

Riley's stomach tightened, nerves waking up again.

In the quiet of the hotel room, when Maria was minding her own business, it was easier to pretend everything was normal. Or, at least, everything wasn't life-and-death.

Maria pulled her pistol out.

"I'm going to untie you and then the same rules apply," she said. "Cute kid and single mom get their lives destroyed or you walk calmly to the car and get in. And before you start wondering what stops you from causing all hell when we're on the road, I just want you to know that I'm going to have backup again." A grin split her contoured face. "And this individual is highly motivated."

Maria stopped talking after that. She didn't untie Riley and Riley didn't feel like talking anymore either. Minutes that felt like hours went by until the sound of a car door shutting made both women turn their heads toward the curtain over the window.

Only one of them ran to it and peered out.

"Finally," Maria breathed.

She leaned against the wall next to the door until someone knocked.

Riley's heartbeat thundered in her chest.

If this wasn't Ryan, who was it?

The man in the suit again?

How was he highly motivated?

"It's about time something happened," Maria greeted after she let the man in. "I'll let you get her untied while I do a refresh on my makeup. Heaven knows this hotel air isn't doing it any favors."

Maria took her purse and disappeared into the bathroom, not bothering to even look at the woman she'd tied up.

Which was good, because Riley was having a hard time keeping her composure.

Evan Davies looked as guilty as sin as he crouched down in front of her. He didn't even flinch at the sight of her tied up.

"What are you doing here?" Riley bit out.

He eyed the first knot he'd been ordered to untie, refusing to meet her stare.

"I'm supposed to take you to meet Ryan."

If Riley's legs had been free she would have kicked him with every ounce of power she had.

"I can't believe this," she seethed. "I can't believe you'd—"

Davies moved in closer and dropped his voice into a whisper. Finally he met her gaze.

"We think Ryan wants to kill Jenna so he can get custody of Hartley and then his inheritance." Riley felt her eyes widen. He kept on. "Ryan has played everything smart enough that nothing will stick to him when this is all over." Davies glanced at the bathroom door. "Which is why Desmond wants to set a trap." At the mention of her cowboy's name, Riley couldn't help but feel relief. It must have shown. Davies's face softened. "If you don't want to we can get you out now, no problem, but if you do want to then you need to play along."

"I'm only in here because Maria has been threatening to kill the owner if I don't cooperate," Riley hurried. "I don't care about me—I just don't want anyone to get hurt."

"Don't worry—we'll have Maria covered. She won't hurt anyone if we do this."

Don't worry was a piece of advice that was hard to take when tied up in a motel room and given by a man who Riley absolutely did not trust anymore.

And maybe Davies realized that too.

"You don't believe in me—I get that," he said quickly. "But I *do* think you believe in him."

"You could be lying," she pointed out.

"Which is why I'm supposed to tell you that after this he said you two could enjoy PB&Js and watch *Wheel of Fortune*."

The sound of the toilet flushing followed by the sink turning on were the only noises that filled the room for a few moments.

Then Riley made a decision.

She didn't trust the man in front of her but she did trust Desmond.

"Okay," she said. "Let's get the bastard."

Chapter Nineteen

Riley hadn't been privy to Desmond's plan but now, less than an hour later, she knew without a doubt that every part of it had gone sideways. The rain had thoroughly soaked their clothes. Which was good, considering it had also washed away most of the blood. Still, the pain was there. It blanketed their bodies and made navigating through the trees even more difficult.

Riley clutched her side; Jenna ran with a heavy limp.

Both were panting from effort; neither was slowing down.

They couldn't. Not when he was still free.

"Ca-Caleb said it's around—around here?" Jenna huffed out.

They had made it to a stream. The trees overhead had thinned letting the rainstorm that had started at the absolutely worst time hit them with ease. Riley shielded her eyes and looked as far down the stream to the left as she could.

"Yeah. Two hundred yards or—or so."

Jenna grunted. She reached out for Riley's hand and they splashed through the water and onto the bank opposite. Then they were running along the tree line.

Riley's body hurt but it was her heart that had taken the biggest blow. The only reason she was as focused as she was on finding the vacation cabin had to do with the woman who was holding her hand.

If Ryan caught Jenna, he would kill her.

That had been made abundantly clear at the barn.

The gunfire and yelling still rang through her head.

Riley didn't know if she'd ever sleep again if that was the nightmare that might appear.

"There," Jenna yelled out. She tugged Riley so hard along with her that the pain in her side from falling temporarily redirected to her arm.

That's when Riley saw the rental, deeper within the trees.

It's a vacation rental. No one is there now, Caleb had hurriedly told them behind their cover. *Break in, hide and try your phones. Cell service there is spotty, though, so if there's no landline then regroup and head out when you think it's safe. Now go!*

The cabin was probably a sanctuary to those who rented it. Set between a mountain and the county road that led to town, and covered by trees, it was a large yet secluded escape. Which would have been nice had they been vacationing. As they ran up the stairs to the wraparound porch, the serenity was eerie.

Jenna went up to the back door. Riley took her hand and pulled her to, and then past, the front door. She went to one of the windows on the opposite side of the stream and out of view from the drive.

"If we're going to break in, let's do it somewhere kind of hidden."

Riley grabbed a bear figurine hanging out on the porch railing and readied to throw it through the glass.

Jenna grabbed her arm to stop her. Wordlessly she pressed her palms against the window and pushed up. The window didn't budge. It was locked. Riley raised her eyebrow at her sister. Jenna motioned to the window and stepped back.

"As you were."

The bear statue shattered the glass on the first throw. Jenna picked up one of the small wooden patio tables along the porch and used its legs to clear the rest of the bottom portion's glass away.

"Be careful," she warned as Riley ducked and went through.

Glass crunched under her shoes.

While she would never think of Maria in any good terms, she was thankful the woman had forced her to change before they'd walked into the motel room, even if it was into one of Maria's work outfits. Apparently walking around in slippers and Jenna's pajamas had been too suspicious even by her standards.

Now Riley was in a drenched blouse, pair of slacks and flats that were too small and bit at her toes.

Not that she was concerned about that minor annoyance at the moment.

"Try your phone," Riley said as soon as Jenna was inside. The room they'd come into was large, vaulted and furnished to the nines. Jenna pulled her phone out and dialed while Riley stepped back onto the glass to grab the curtains. She pulled them over the window hoping that it wouldn't make the broken window as noticeable from the outside.

"I have no bars here," Jenna said after a moment.

"Keep trying and look for a landline!"

Riley clutched at her side as the pain reminded her she'd been hurt and hurried to the back door. It was off a small hall at the rear of the kitchen, attached to the living area. She peeked out the window through the top half of the door. The rain had died way down and the sun was already starting to show again.

Riley hoped it stayed that way.

She was glad to see no one coming through the trees after them.

"I'm going upstairs to see if that helps," Jenna called. "There's no landline down here."

"Hurry!"

Riley didn't know where the stairs were but she heard Jenna pound up them.

Then she was alone.

Riley leaned against the door and fought the urge to squeeze her eyes closed and cry.

This was all a nightmare. Every second since Desmond had warned her someone was in his house. Sure, there had been hope within that nightmare. Hope that they'd catch Ryan so he wouldn't be able to weasel his way out of everything. Hope that he'd finally pay for what he'd done and spend the rest of his life behind bars.

That hope had only grown when Davies had taken them to the barn out on someone's—she still had no idea who that person was, though—property and there had been Desmond.

Even with Desmond on his knees, face bloodied and bruised and a gun pointed at him, Riley had felt that hope well in her chest at being near him.

Then that hope had turned hot. She'd been scared that Davies had lied.

That's when she'd realized who it was pointing the gun at him.

Julian Mercer had been dressed in a suit meant to impress and had looked absolutely terrifying.

Maria hadn't flinched in the slightest at the sight of him.

I have to admit, I'm more impressed with the men in suits for their sense of style rather than their cunning, she'd noted before they'd gotten out.

That's when Riley had really believed their plan might work. Maria had taken one look at the intimidating appearance of Desmond's brother-in-law and had assumed he was on her side, just as the man in the suit had been at Desmond's house earlier.

Just as she had trusted Davies wasn't lying to her.

But then…

Then Ryan had shown up.

And then everything had gone wrong.

Riley's vision started to blur. Jenna's footfalls coming down the stairs made her straighten again but there was no fooling her sister. Jenna's eyes softened, even as she gave the bad news.

"Caleb's right. I can't get any call out but I hit Send on texts to Dorothy's and Madi's phones. If we hit a pocket of service hopefully they'll go through. I never found a landline."

"Dorothy and Madi know you're here?"

Jenna looked guilty as all get-out.

"No. No one knew," she admitted. "I nearly gave Desmond a heart attack when I popped up in his back seat once we left the ranch."

Riley opened her mouth to scold her sister when Jenna moved directly in front of her.

It was the first time they'd had any chance to

have a conversation since Maria and the man in the suit had come for her.

"I understand why you switched places with me. And now I need you to understand why I had to go out to that barn." She put her hand flat over her heart. They hadn't had a moment to talk about the plan or the barn they'd all found themselves at before everything wrong had happened. "Twin or not, you and Hartley are my heart. There's no me without you two. So there was no force on this earth that would keep me from trying to help take down the man who is trying to take you both. I love you, Riley Lee, but you're just plain stupid if you think I was going to sit this one out."

"What about Hartley?"

Jenna didn't waver in her resolve.

"He's with Madi. I may have let myself down when it came to my relationship with Ryan but I wasn't about to do the same for Hartley. When Desmond and Davies told me what he was most likely after, I convinced Madi to let me record a video on her phone just in case. I detailed everything Ryan ever did to me, how he'd never shown real love to Hartley and how in the event of my death and your death that his home would be with Mom and Dad. Madi swore if anything happened to us that the entire Nash family would make sure that wish was held up." She smiled. It was small. "And, I'll be honest, I believe that they would fight for us even though we're not technically family."

"Did you call Mom and Dad?" Riley asked, even though she knew the answer already.

Jenna shook her head.

"They'd be on the first flight out. If everything went sideways I didn't want them getting caught in the cross fire."

"Smart," Riley had to agree. "Especially since everything *did* go sideways."

Riley's vision started to blur again as tears rimmed her eyes. This time Jenna put her arms around her.

"He could still be okay," she tried to assure. "They all could still be alright."

But Riley heard the uncertainty in her statement.

Just as she heard the footsteps on the porch outside.

Riley turned to the window, hoping that just thinking about Desmond had conjured him.

Her heart broke all over again.

It wasn't Desmond. It wasn't Julian. It wasn't Caleb.

It wasn't even Davies or Maria.

It was Ryan Alcaster.

And he still had his gun.

"Madi is going to be so pissed."

Caleb had lost too much blood. He was pale and it had nothing to do with how soaked they were from the rain or their jaunt in the river. Julian must have thought the same. He shared a worried look with Desmond after they had helped him from the water and into the trees.

The barn was in the distance, mocking them.

No one had followed them.

Then again, there had been little left to interpret after Ryan and the men with him had unloaded a barrage of bullets in their direction.

They all should have been dead.

They all *would* have been had they not been faster into the water.

Then again, not all of them had been fast enough.

Julian was bleeding heavily from the split in his head thanks to the fight he'd gotten into with one of the men who had come with Ryan. The crimson was a shock against Julian's tan skin and one of the reasons Desmond hadn't noticed that his own graze from earlier had opened and had bled through his shirt.

Neither wound could compare to Caleb's.

"Why is Madi going to be pissed?" Desmond asked, crouching next to his brother. Julian followed suit. He didn't ask for permission as he ripped open Caleb's pant leg.

"Because now she's the only Nash sibling who hasn't been shot."

Desmond hated seeing the bullet wound in Caleb's leg just as much as he'd hated hearing him yell out before they had jumped off the raised bank overhang and made it into the water. Julian, a former marine, was all analytical as he inspected it. His voice was nothing but calm when he spoke.

"And we're going to let her stay mad because that's never going to happen." He motioned to Desmond. "Give me your belt. I need to make a tourniquet or he's going to bleed out."

Desmond ripped his belt off and handed it over feeling the terrible weight of helplessness press against him. Caleb watched the move. Then he looked to the river.

"Remember when I fished Declan and Nina out of that river?" His voice was strained.

"It's about the only two things you can say you caught in there," Desmond replied, trying to smile. "Because you sure never caught any fish."

Caleb chuckled. Then he winced.

Julian adjusted the belt around his thigh.

"Hold him down."

Desmond didn't have to be told twice.

His brother let out a terrible cry of pain as Julian twisted the belt tight.

"He might pass out but that's okay," Julian warned.

"I'm still here, big guy," Caleb said.

Julian kept quiet as he kept turning. Desmond had his arm wrapped around Caleb's chest. Before he finished Desmond felt his body go limp.

"It's the pain," Julian answered his unspoken fear. "He's lost a lot of blood but this should help him remain stable for a bit. He needs medical attention now."

Julian pulled his phone out. It was wet.

"Let's see if this is actually waterproof like they claim."

Desmond patted his brother on the chest and slipped out from under him. He pointed to the trees behind them as Julian dialed.

"County 11 is a half mile that way. If you can walk him there it'll save the ambulance a lot of time getting back here."

Julian nodded, nonplussed at the idea of carrying a full-grown, unconscious man a half mile through the woods while soaking wet, hurt and in the rain. Then again, he was their very own gentle giant.

"You're going to the rental Caleb told the women about?" he asked, already putting the phone between his ear and shoulder and positioning himself to pick up Caleb.

"Yeah, and I'm not waiting for backup to get here."

Julian snorted.

"If it was Madi, I wouldn't let some jerk like me tell me not to go." He gave Desmond a deep nod. "If you get the chance, take them out one by one. Stealth is strength's enemy when used right."

Whoever he called answered the phone and

that was that. Julian threw Caleb over his shoulder like a rag doll and took off at a jog.

Desmond didn't waste any of his time either. He ran back to the river and followed it. The overhang of raised grass and dirt gave him cover until he was near the barn. He climbed up, slipping on the dirt turned to mud in the rain, and was met with the sight of bullet holes, abandoned vehicles and bodies.

If Desmond hadn't been part of the distraction that had allowed Riley and Jenna to disappear into the woods, he would have had ice in his stomach.

Instead, he walked past a man in slacks and a blazer who he didn't recognize lying motionless on the ground, Maria with her eyes open and staring up at the sky and Davies across from her.

Desmond only paused by the first man long enough to grab the gun at his feet.

The SUV Ryan and the three men had driven up in was still parked next to the road while they were nowhere to be found.

Which meant they must have followed Riley and Jenna into the woods.

Desmond took off running, limp be damned.

Chapter Twenty

Riley was so terrified and mad and frustrated, she didn't know which emotion to jump in and soak up. Instead she took a little of each.

"We should have grabbed one of the guns," she said at Jenna's ear as they hurried up the stairs that were tucked away at the opposite side of the living room. There was a loft lounge area that opened up to the front of the house and a hallway that branched off in both directions from it.

"I *did* have one but after Ryan shot Maria I just—" Jenna didn't finish the thought. While neither had been a fan of the woman, it had been absolutely horrible to watch the bullet hit her in the chest. And, perhaps even worse, the betrayal and pain that had crossed her face as she realized the man she loved had been the one to do it.

Not only had he pulled the trigger, he'd smiled.

It was an awful end for anyone.

Riley knew it would haunt her and Jenna for a long time to come.

That is, if the same madman didn't find them first.

"We need to hide," Riley said, choosing the hallway to the left.

"Hard to do when we're trailing water and mud," Jenna whispered.

Riley looked back the way they'd come.

She was right.

The rain had been light when Ryan had pulled up. After he'd shot Maria and his friends had surprised them the bottom had dropped out.

It had created more chaos that only made seeing what happened to the rest of their friends harder.

The gunshots, the yelling, the splintering of wood.

Then nothing but the rain.

Just as fast as it had come over them, it had started to ebb.

Now it was still managing to make everything worse. The runner along the hardwood floors on the second-floor landing had collected the water still coming off their hair, clothes and shoes. Hiding was going to be impossible.

"They're going to know exactly where we go."

"*If* they come inside."

"This is the only place for miles," Riley hissed back. "Of course they're going to come in."

A small puddle of water was already pooling

around them as they spoke. Riley decided on a bad idea.

"Strip down," she hurried, already ripping open Maria's blouse and stepping out of her shoes. "They might find us but we're not going to make it easy."

Riley didn't know if Jenna would have agreed with the plan had a terrifying sound not floated up to them from the first floor.

Shattering glass.

Jenna's eyes widened.

Then her shirt was off in a flash.

STEALTH.

Not something any of the people Desmond was following had used.

From the bank of the stream all the way to the wraparound porch of the vacation rental, there were muddy footprints. It was a blessing and a concern all at the same time.

Following the men to stop them was made easier, sure, but based on two sets of smaller prints he saw every few feet, the women's footprints had been easy to follow too.

Desmond checked that the safety was off on the gun in his hand. He made sure it was loaded too. He'd never wanted to shoot anyone in his life and yet he'd already shot Geordi Green and, he believed, the man at the clearing. Caleb had shot one of the men who was with Ryan too.

At least, he hoped it was one of the bad guys because, mixed in with the mud, was a decent amount of blood.

He wasn't built like a house like Julian but if it was Riley or Jenna who was hurt, he was going to throw them over his shoulder and walk them to safety too.

No one was going to stop him.

Desmond slowed as he made it to the corner of the back side of the house. No footsteps were visible across the stones that led to the front.

Stealth was strength's enemy.

Solid advice from Julian.

Advice Desmond was going to take.

He kept low and hurried along the side of the raised porch. The rain had stopped. He strained to hear any movement inside.

Someone was talking. A man.

Desmond stopped, crouching next to the stairs that led to the front door, and firmly ignored the pain radiating up his leg. If he had to, he'd crawl his way to end this.

He slowed his breathing, felt the weight of the gun in his hand and peered around the wooden railing. The front door was open, the window at its side broken. Desmond could see movement through it.

At least one of the gunmen from earlier was inside the house.

Desmond readied himself, muscles and pain

thrumming in anticipation, when a figure walked around the other side of the house.

It was the man in the suit who had taken Riley that morning from his house. Even soaked, his clothes were immaculate. It made the gun he had aimed at Desmond even more intimidating.

He pressed his finger to his lips.

Desmond was about to get to shooting bad guys earlier than intended when the man moved his hand to a stop motion. Then lowered his gun.

"We need to talk," he said, loud enough for Desmond to hear but not enough that the men inside came out.

Desmond pulled his gun up and aimed. He didn't shoot.

Part of him was ready to pull the trigger. The same part that had been hit hard enough to lose consciousness. The same part that had failed so that Riley could be taken from *his* house.

The other part wasn't as quick to jump the literal gun.

That part was reading the body language of the man and remembering how he'd kept Maria from shooting him or Riley.

That part was also quite aware that the man wasn't calm and collected as he had been in the house.

He was angry.

And it wasn't at Desmond.

"Slowly," he warned as the man kept low and

made his way over. He stopped on the other side of the stairs. He made no move for his gun once there.

"Ryan Alcaster is in there with two of my guys," the man stated. Desmond hadn't read the man wrong. There was anger in his words.

"Anyone else?" Desmond ventured, fishing to see if he knew about the women.

"A set of twins who have a lot more spunk than I gave either credit for."

Desmond felt his jaw harden. His trigger finger was itching.

"Sounds like getting you out of the picture makes things a little easier for me then."

The man eyed the gun and then got down to business.

"I'm here to help even the playing field, not add to it."

Desmond snorted, glanced at the door and shook his head.

"I don't believe you."

That annoyed the man.

"Ryan Alcaster broke the terms of our agreement," he said with a growl. "The person I work for doesn't take that lightly."

"So what does that mean for him and the Stone sisters?" Desmond motioned between them. "You're just going to let me go in there and shoot your own people?"

The sun was back in the sky, uncovered by the

clouds. It bathed the front half of the house next to them in light. It also gave Desmond the clearest view of the man he'd seen so far.

Tall, well built and custom tailored. His hair was on the longer side of short and well kept. There was no stubble above his lip or against his jaw. A youthfulness rang from his quick and fluid movements but there was an aged wariness that circled his eyes. They were dark gray, much like the cloud that had moved on with the storm.

Desmond didn't recognize him at all.

Not a hint. Not a whisper.

But then he saw the scar on his hand.

Suddenly Desmond was eight again.

The man who had taken them had had that same scar. An *X* on the skin between the knuckles of his thumb and index finger and his wrist. Such a small but memorable detail. One of the only details the triplets had remembered that had made their abductor stand out.

Caleb, especially, had been affected by that scar. He'd admitted to Desmond that it had taken him years until he stopped looking for that scar on every man he met.

Now here Desmond was seeing it for the first time since he was a terrified and hurt kid living a nightmare.

Yet the man with the same scar wasn't the same man.

But he sure enough recognized the connection

Desmond had just made. He glanced at his hand and then used it to point to the house.

"The man you managed to shoot out near the barn was an idiot, but my other two men in there are not. They're good shots, which is why I'm assuming you and Mr. Mercer are still in good shape. Those two knew not to shoot you," he said. A flash of anger moved across his face, tensing a muscle in his forehead. "Ryan is the one who hit Caleb and that's exactly what broke the rules." He jabbed his index finger in the air again toward the house. "You can sit here and ask me questions. Then shoot me and try to go in there and put two highly trained men down and hope you can deal with the egotistical maniac before he kills your girlfriend and her sister *or* I can walk in there right now and make my men leave with me. But, either way, we're both running out of time. I know the cavalry is on their way and Ryan has been in that house for at least two minutes."

He dropped his hand to his side again. Desmond watched as the scar shaped like an *X* went with it.

"So what will it be, Desmond? Me or the redheads?"

The Nash triplet abduction had consumed every part of the Nash family's lives since that interrupted game of hide-and-seek all those years ago. He'd given Riley his version of what had happened and how it had affected him but he hadn't told her everything.

He hadn't told her how it had cracked a marriage that should have withstood decades.

He hadn't told her how it had taken a good, honest man and made him lose faith in the world around him, seeing ghosts where there were none and creating his own personal demons that eventually saw to the end of him.

He hadn't told her how it had convinced Declan he was somehow responsible and in turn put him in a profession that held nothing but responsibility to everyone but himself, making a happy boy ready for the future into a man who toed the line between justice and obsession as their father had.

He hadn't told her how it had created a rage within Madi. One that had burned so hot that an invisible ring of fire had kept anyone and everyone away from her for years, driving her slowly into self-imposed isolation.

He hadn't told her that, while Caleb had tried his best to live a happier life, he'd subconsciously marched right into his father's old one, hell-bent on finding the answer to every mystery no matter the cost.

He hadn't told her that the real reason he had gone into business in the beginning was to make enough money so that he could buy the world. Buy *their* world. The one in which the story of the Nash family abduction was common knowledge. The one that they'd all never really left. And, only then, have every tool imaginable to find out the truth of what happened.

Because, one thing the Nash triplets and Declan hadn't told anyone was that they were all still waiting for the second shoe to drop.

They were all still those scared children, at least in part, and probably always would be. At least, until they found the man who took them.

The man with the scar on his hand.

He hadn't told Riley any of this but, in that moment, staring at the first clue they'd had in over a decade, Desmond realized he'd already planned to tell her one day.

In the future. In *their* future.

So, there wasn't an option. Not really. Not for Desmond.

He looked the man in the suit in the eyes and had never been more sure in his decision than he was now.

"I choose the redheads."

There was surprise in the man's expression but he didn't waste any more time talking. He stood, kept his gun down and walked up the stairs. Desmond followed, a firm grip on his own weapon. They walked right through the open front door like they were ready to start their vacation.

A man wearing a black blazer spun to face them. Desmond worried he'd made a mistake at the sight of his gun. Yet the second his eyes settled on the man in the suit, he lowered it.

Another man, dressed nicely as well, walked from the back of the room with widened eyes.

"We're leaving," the man in the suit said to both of them. His voice carried despite his lowered tone. Desmond glanced around to see if Ryan was there.

He wasn't.

He also wasn't in the loft space on the second floor.

It made his gut twist.

"He wasn't supposed to shoot anyone," the man said, coming closer. He looked like a scared child tattling on another child to avoid getting into trouble. "We told him not to but he hit one of them."

The man in the suit nodded.

"Which is why we're leaving. Now."

The lackey kept his eyes widened but didn't complain. He was out the front door in a flash. As the one in the blazer went to follow, Desmond stopped him.

"Where are the women?"

The man looked at his boss who gave a quick nod.

"Hiding somewhere in here. Alcaster has been cussing going through the rooms."

Desmond didn't dare feel relief. Not until he could see Riley. *Touch* her. Know she was safe.

The man followed his friend out. His boss hung back a second.

"We both know that the only way to stop a man like Alcaster from coming back is to kill him."

Then he left too.

Chapter Twenty-One

Their plan had been simple.

Two of the bedrooms upstairs were connected by a Jack-and-Jill bathroom. When Ryan and his unmerry men came into the first bedroom Riley and Jenna would be listening at the bathroom and then fall back to the other bedroom and slip out into the hallway and leave.

If the men split up and searched the bedrooms at the same time, they'd use the bathroom to hide.

If the men decided to search the bathroom at the same time, effectively cutting off their options for escape, while they were hiding in it?

Well, they were screwed.

A simple plan with a simple conclusion.

But, it wasn't like Riley or Jenna had many options. Once they'd stripped down to their underwear—with Riley thanking every god that might exist that she'd put her panties and bra back on after she'd showered with Desmond, scared that his mother would somehow show up again—and thrown the clothes and shoes out of view in the corner of the loft, they'd barely had the time to slip into the first bedroom.

Considering the jump from the second story to the ground was too high, there were no roof overhangs, and no weapons, makeshift or otherwise, unless you counted pillows with embroidered sunsets and a myriad of white linen towels, they weren't escaping or fighting their way out. At least not with any good odds in their favor. So, they'd taken to their simple yet extremely easy-to-foil plan with vigor.

Which was why they were presently in the room farthest from the loft, Riley with her ear to the bathroom door and Jenna with her ear to the hallway door. For what felt like hours neither did so much as breathe.

Then Jenna started to point wildly at her door.

She hurriedly went to Riley and together, as quietly as they could, they slipped into the bathroom.

Riley's heart was in her throat and she closed the door behind them. Unlike the bedroom doors, these locked. That didn't mean anything when it came to bullets but it would slow them down. Riley twisted the lock and they hurried through the next door.

Then they were standing in the other bedroom.

When Ryan started laughing from just inside the bedroom door, gun aimed at them, they didn't even have time to scream.

"Move and I shoot one of you," Ryan announced around his smile. "I don't care which at this point so may that keep the other one of you from doing anything dumb for fear of me taking out your beloved twin."

Riley was prepared to angle herself in front of Jenna when Jenna instead pushed against her shoulder. It was a subtle move that meant she didn't want Riley to do exactly what she was going to do.

Ryan motioned to the door they'd just come through and laughed again.

"By the way, that little attempt at a trick to get past me was what you used to do with Hartley when you played hide-and-seek." He surprised Riley by addressing Jenna without hesitation. That shock must have shown. He glanced down at Riley's thigh. "And may I take a moment to say thank you for your impulsiveness. It makes telling you two apart much easier."

Riley had never in her life been so mad at herself for getting a tattoo. She didn't have time to bask in that anger for too long.

Ryan was a talkative man. He was used to walking into a room and commanding it. Just as he had thought he should be able to command a wife. Even now, in such an intense situation that was so far from a boardroom or cocktail party, he was raring to capture their attention.

To be entertaining.

To talk.

To hear his own voice.

Riley couldn't believe she'd ever thought any nice thing about the man. She'd once called him handsome with his thick, dark hair, sharp facial features and jade-green eyes. She'd once been impressed with his unwavering confidence and smarts. She'd once been enamored at how wonderfully he'd treated her sister.

Now every opinion had twisted into the *thing* that stood no more than a few feet from them.

"I have to say, the last few weeks have been a bit of a headache. Who knew either of you had it in you to be so much of an obstacle. I certainly didn't." He shook his head. "Do you know how much I've had to pay just to make it all look like Maria went insane? A lot of money. More than either one of you is worth, I can tell you that."

"You wanted to kill me and blame it on your mistress?"

Jenna's voice bit as she asked the question. Ryan's smile moved into a smirk.

"Oh no, my darling Jenna, that was plan C." He looked at Riley. "Thanks to this one switching places with you *and* Brett's idiocy, I had to make a new contract with my nicely dressed friends. But then, when you weren't busy messing everything up, your poor, lovesick ex-husband had to try to sabotage me." He snorted. "Davies was a good guy but he's never had the strength to know his place about the likes of you. Even after you abandoned him he still ran after you like some whipped little pup. Disgusting, if you ask me."

"So you manipulated Maria to go right where you wanted her to be," Riley guessed.

He nodded.

"Maria had many assets I'll be sad to lose but one I appreciated the most was her willingness to listen to what I had to say without question." He cut his eyes to Jenna. "A trait we both know you never possessed."

Riley grabbed Jenna's arm. It was more to keep her from springing forward and wiping the smugness from the man they both once thought they knew. Just as it was also to keep Riley from doing the same. If they attacked him when he was so close, there was no doubt in her mind that he'd shoot at least one of them.

And Riley couldn't be sure it wouldn't be Jenna. Just as she was sure Jenna knew the bullet might hit Riley.

It was the perfect way to keep them both in line.

"So what was the plan? Your girlfriend goes crazy, terrorizes your ex-wife and kills a bunch of people?" Riley asked.

"That was the idea. Until that pathetic puppy Davies decided to team up with the most annoying family in the world."

"But then you shot him and Maria."

Riley replayed the scene in her head again. It still made her stomach knot.

Ryan had gotten out to talk to Maria, Julian and Desmond who was playing the part of captive. The plan, as far as Riley could tell, had been to catch the man in the act of issuing the deaths of Jenna and Desmond in front of Julian, Davies and Caleb, who was lurking behind the cars.

But then Ryan had shocked them all by shooting the two people who had been and pretended to be on his side.

If Jenna hadn't have sprung out and pulled Riley aside in time, he would have ended her too.

"There were too many players in the game," Ryan replied. "So I shelled out some more money to get more of a team willing to play for me and started to clean shop. My girlfriend killing my ex and your ex killing you *and* your new lover? Honestly, that would have been perfect. But this story is still writing itself. Between Maria and Davies? I can just switch their roles. Either way it's all about exes killing exes. And who doesn't like a story about that?"

He looked around the room.

"It doesn't matter where the end of it happens. I'm untouchable. And I'll be even more so when my son is back in my custody."

Riley tightened her grip on Jenna.

"You're insane if you think you'll ever get him," she roared, maternal glory coming to the forefront. "Once again your hubris has fooled you into thinking that you're a god when you're not even a man."

Rage, the kind he used to hide behind closed doors, flashed across Ryan's face. His hand tightened on the gun.

"Listen here you little—"

"Move and I'll shoot."

Riley's very own cowboy moved into the room behind Ryan with gun raised and face made of stone.

Riley dropped her hold on Jenna's arm only for Jenna to grab her hand. She squeezed it as Desmond issued his command again.

Ryan's anger at Jenna smoothed away.

It was alarming.

"I'm assuming by Riley's reaction that Desmond Nash is behind me?"

Desmond didn't take his eyes off the back of Ryan's head.

"All you need to know is I'll have no problem shooting you if it means saving them." His baritone was thrumming with authority. The sound wrapped around Riley like an invisible safety blanket.

Ryan started to smirk. His gun was still raised. Now it was pointed at Riley.

"If you shoot me this close to them, I'm afraid your bullet would find a second, unwanted target. The women would need to move. *But* the second they do I'll shoot and then *you'll* shoot and that will probably just kill whichever twin I didn't. You see, it's all just a mess that starts and ends with you trying to save them."

Ryan was right. They were too close. It was too much of a risk. Desmond finally met her eye. The smallest pinch of warmth spread at the fact he looked at her and stayed looking at her. Riley believed then that the world could be ending around them and Desmond would still be able to know which sister she was.

"That silence you hear? That's the sound of an impasse," Ryan added.

Desmond tilted his head to the left. Jenna squeezed her hand. Whether it was a bond created because they were twins, best friends, or just two half-naked women in a bad situation trying to make it out alive, Riley knew exactly what the Stone sisters were about to do.

She gave the smallest of nods to Desmond.

It did not go unnoticed.

"It looks like I've found the sister I'm—" Ryan started.

Desmond didn't let him finish.

Riley lunged to the left as Jenna lunged in sync to the right.

However, the gunshot that sounded afterward was followed by glass shattering and not by Ryan in pain.

RILEY SCRAMBLED INTO the open bathroom and spun around to see Jenna throw herself over the bed. Another gunshot went off and exploded into the wall next to the newly broken window.

The sound of a scuffle ensued.

Riley backpedaled and turned toward the other door. She unlocked it and hightailed it through the adjoining bedroom and back out into the hall.

Just in time to see Desmond and Ryan tumble into the hallway.

"Run," Desmond yelled out as he grabbed Ryan's arm.

Riley's stomach turned to ice as she realized he still had his gun but Desmond didn't. When Ryan saw her he kicked out of Desmond's grip like a bucking bronco.

One second went by where Ryan was completely free.

It was all the time he needed to take aim at Riley and pull the trigger.

Riley closed her eyes on reflex, waiting for the pain.

She thought about her sister and parents and Hartley. About the Nash family, Marty McLinnon, and she even thought about Davies.

The last person who flashed in her mind's eye, however, was the most detailed of all.

Desmond Nash in his cowboy hat, giving her that charming smile that made her stomach flutter.

Riley waited for her end but, after a moment, felt nothing but the chill of being half-naked and wet.

She opened her eyes, confused.

"No!"

Desmond dropped to the floor with a sickening *thud*.

"No!"

Riley lost every sense of self-preservation she had and ran right at her former brother-in-law. When he raised his gun again at her, she didn't even flinch.

When he pulled the trigger and the sound of an empty chamber sang through the hallway, she didn't slow down either.

When Jenna came out in the hallway behind Riley with Desmond's gun in her hand and shot over her sister's shoulder, Riley didn't miss a beat.

Ryan yelled out in shock and ducked into the first bedroom he'd surprised them in earlier. Riley made it to Desmond's side and crouched, tears already in her eyes.

She rolled him over, forgetting about the world around them.

Baby blues stared up at her. His expression was pained but he was alive.

"Pistol in—in my ankle holster," he hurried, wheezing in the middle. "Get—get him."

Getting Ryan had, up until that point, been about saving her sister and her nephew. Now it was for Desmond too.

Rejuvenated by his request, Riley found his ankle holster and took the small pistol out of it. She turned around and met Jenna's wide eyes.

They didn't need to say anything out loud.

Moving in sync once again they ran into the bedrooms that were next to them and then right up to the opened bathroom doors.

Ryan Alcaster was caught between them, standing next to the tub without any options left.

He looked from one sister with a gun pointing at him to the other sister with a gun pointing at him.

His face, his confidence, his ego came crashing down.

When Jenna spoke she did so with a wonderful amount of sass.

"What's wrong, dear? Are you seeing double?"

The real Ryan, the nasty, manipulative and abusive Ryan, opened his mouth to say something. Then he decided against it. Lost for words.

"You know, I was really hoping *someone* would say something clever and twin-related."

Desmond's weight pressed around her as he leaned between her and the door frame. He took the gun from her hand as she examined his chest.

The bullet had torn through his shirt yet there was no blood.

"What?" was all she could manage to ask.

Desmond smiled.

"We might not have included Declan in our

plan just in case everything went wrong but that didn't mean we walked in unprepared." Riley took a closer look at his shirt. There was something black against his chest.

"You're wearing a bulletproof vest," Jenna exclaimed.

He gave her a scolding look.

"We all were and *you would have been wearing one too* had we known you were coming."

Riley couldn't help but throw her arms around the man. He didn't drop the gun but he did groan.

"I'm pretty sure some ribs are broken so watch out."

Riley immediately let go.

"You took another bullet for us," Riley realized.

Desmond's face softened.

"And I would have done it without the vest in a heartbeat too."

Ryan made an annoyed noise.

Desmond was back to angry.

"And you are going to go away for a very, very long time," he said.

Ryan actually laughed. It wasn't as powerful as when he had the upper hand.

"People like me don't go away," he said. "Not when money talks a more convincing game."

This time Desmond was the one to laugh.

"You know, my brother and I talked about that. About you and your money and your seemingly unending influence over people ready to do your bidding. Riley, can you reach into my pocket and pull out my cell phone?"

Riley obliged, confused.

Until she saw what was on the screen.

"So before we left for the barn all of us cleared our phones and started to hit Record the second you pulled up. And the best part about the app we used? It doesn't need service or internet to keep working. Riley, is it still going?"

"Yes. It is."

Jenna made a noise. Tears were falling down her cheeks.

They had him.

They had Ryan.

And he knew it.

He didn't say another word.

Desmond, however, had to get in one last jab.

"You gotta love technology, huh?"

Epilogue

"Desmond?"

The house was quiet. Riley stared at the bed, her stomach knotted.

"Desmond?" she tried again, raising her voice.

This time his baritone made its way up the stairs to her.

"I don't know what she's wearing yet! She hasn't gotten out of the car!"

Riley shook her head and focused on the different outfits spread out on the cowboy's bed. The first outfit was casual but put-together, jeans and a button-down. The last outfit was a finely pressed, stylish blouse and pencil skirt. There were three cowgirl hats in different colors sitting on the pillows, courtesy of the Nash downstairs.

Riley tapped her bare foot against the rug. The AC she'd been praising for the last month was now making her cold. Then again, she *was* standing in her underwear beneath a vent.

It was now June in Overlook and summer had more than made its way to town. In the five months between Ryan being arrested and now, a lot had changed.

And a lot hadn't.

Like that flutter that danced in her stomach when Desmond smiled, even when she just heard it in his voice from the other room.

"Outfit number two," he yelled after another moment. "Outfit number two!"

Riley heard this as the man ran up the stairs and into his bedroom. Or what would be theirs starting next week after they finished moving the last of her stuff in. Bless the man, he was good at so many things, but when it came to moving her book collection and winter clothes he'd gotten right near grumpy. It probably hadn't helped that Jenna had stopped him countless times to open the box he was carrying and steal out an item or two.

"She's wearing dark jeans and a frilly top," Desmond said almost out of breath. He motioned to his shirt. "You know, kind of like that one you wore last week when we went to the Red Oak with Marty and his husband."

Riley nodded, touched Desmond always remembered the details, and shimmied into a pair of nice jeans and one of Jenna's red blouses that *she'd* managed to steal when Jenna was stealing from her.

"Was she wearing flats or—"

"Cowboy boots."

Riley ran to the closet and pulled out a pair Madi had gifted to her for her birthday. Jenna had gotten a matching pair and she and Riley, in the privacy of Jenna's room, had put them on and danced around in them while yelling "Yeehaw." Their mother, who had flown in with their dad to celebrate the twins' birthday, had insisted on buying her own pair too. Hartley, naturally, already had a pair.

"Okay, how do I look?" Riley asked, spinning around when she was done.

She was met with *that* smile. One that often preceded both of them having a very good time.

"You said I can't call you perfect because it doesn't exist but I just can't find another word." He closed the distance between them and dipped her down for a brief but powerful kiss. She laughed against him and then struggled to regain her composure.

"But does it say, *Hire me to manage your social media and website because I've got great ideas, the know-how, and work with my brilliant designer sister*?"

Desmond laughed. The doorbell rang.

"Claire already hired you, babe," he pointed out. "And she asked to come here just to talk about some ideas. You don't need to worry."

Riley let out a long breath.

"I know but, well, sometimes I can't help it."

Desmond swung low again and kissed her. Then he was headed for the door in a rush.

"If you really want to impress her, wear the gray Stetson," he called over his shoulder. "You know, the one that makes me *wild*!"

Riley couldn't help but laugh at that. She waited a beat, looked at her reflection over the dresser with an encouraging nod to herself and followed the same steps the man she loved had just taken.

But only after she grabbed the cowgirl hat.

THE BREEZE WAS NICE and so was the company.

Desmond sat atop Winona as she walked back toward the stables in the distance. Declan, on his horse Rocky, matched their pace next to them.

They'd ridden the ranch's fence perimeter together in companionable silence but now it felt like time to talk. While both men enjoyed riding as a solo adventure most of the time, there was just something to be said about enjoying it with family.

"I saw Claire pull up to the house earlier," Declan started in. "Ma said she's Riley's newest client?"

Desmond nodded, proud.

"Yep. Her third so far in Overlook, actually. Apparently our small town is great at word of mouth but not so great at marketing on the internet. After the work she and Jenna have done with

Second Wind, it's been a no-brainer for people to hire them."

"I'm glad they're doing what they love too. It sure makes a difference. I ran into Jenna at the store earlier and she practically was lighting the place up with how much she was smiling."

Desmond nodded in agreement.

Jenna had completely broken down in relief when Declan and his deputies had arrived at the vacation rental after both women had stopped Ryan from fleeing. The recording, plus eyewitnesses of what had happened at the barn, had been enough to send Ryan to prison for life. There was no way he'd ever get out and there was no way he'd ever get Hartley.

That fact, plus being surrounded by people who genuinely cared for and respected her, had finally allowed her to start healing from Ryan's abuse.

In turn, an invisible weight had seemed to lift from Riley too. It was helped by her finally getting some closure she said she hadn't realized she'd needed from Davies. While Ryan had killed Maria, Davies had survived his wounds. Riley had stayed with him at the hospital until his sister had arrived. Before then he'd finally apologized for his silence about Ryan and Jenna. He'd even told what he knew of the abuse on the stand at the trial against Ryan. It had been another nail in the businessman's coffin.

After that, life in Overlook had gone back to as normal as it ever got. Caleb started physical therapy and had improved to almost new. Nina and he had made it no secret how thankful they were for what Julian had done to save him, and when they announced that Nina was pregnant with a baby boy, they also announced that the boy's middle name would match the man who had saved his father.

Julian, the mountain of the man he was, had teared up at the honor. Madi had all but cried.

Between the barn incident and now, Desmond had spent his time making sure the red-haired siren had known he had fallen for her hook, line and sinker. Riley moving in was only the beginning.

What she didn't know, but her father did, was that Desmond was already planning on popping the question.

He intended on talking to Jenna about it later that night after dinner. Because, if there was one thing he knew about the sisters with absolute certainty, it was that you didn't get one without the other.

Desmond actually loved that about them because it was exactly how he felt when it came to his family.

As for his big brother, riding next to him with the obvious weight of the world on his shoulders, Desmond was a little worried. Everyone was getting their happy endings while Declan was only getting more and more into his work.

Even now, with the sun shining and the breeze blowing, there was something he was holding on to that Desmond couldn't see.

So, he asked.

"You know, I think you've looked worried since the day we got Ryan Alcaster. What's wrong? We got the bad guy."

Declan didn't bother denying the accusation.

"We got Ryan, Maria and *a* man in a suit. But we didn't get *the* man, did we?"

It was true. The man Desmond had shot outside the barn had succumbed to his injuries, and with his death whatever secrets he had were also gone. They'd never been able to ID him. The man with the scar on his hand had also disappeared. There had been no trace of him at all.

Declan had said he wasn't actively looking anymore.

Desmond suspected that was a lie.

His older brother let out a long sigh.

"It's just that every time we think we're getting back to normal around here something *bizarre* happens. How much bad luck can we have before it stops being bad luck and becomes a pattern?"

"We also deal with danger in our everyday careers, even by proxy, more than most," Desmond pointed out. "You and Caleb *are* in law enforcement after all."

Declan conceded but with a slight caveat.

"And I could stomach that, and even chalk up the man in the suit not wanting to kill any of the Nashes because of the spotlight it could be on them as a group, if it wasn't for the man at the bar."

Desmond had to think on that.

Declan explained before he could figure it out.

"When we caught who had targeted Nina and Caleb, they said a man at the bar gave them the idea to do it. When Madi was targeted, the idea was also from a man in a bar." Desmond felt the tightness of realization and worry zip through him.

"And Ryan Alcaster said at his trial that a stranger in a bar gave him the idea to use his girlfriend to get back at his ex-wife," he finished.

Declan nodded, brow creased in a thought he didn't particular like.

"One mention of a man in a bar I can let roll off my shoulders. Two mentions of a man in a bar is a coincidence that makes me pause, but three?"

"What are you thinking?"

"I'm thinking it feels like someone is pulling a set of strings we can't see," he said. "Like someone is three steps away from taking out our king while we're just now figuring out we're even pieces on a game board." He rolled his shoulders back and patted Rocky. They were almost to the stables. "Caleb first, Madi second and now you."

Neither man voiced it, but if there was a pattern, it meant that Decl
an could be next. A thought that darkened the mood even further.

"It *could* be nothing," Desmond tried. "I think it's easy for this family to feel targeted, to feel attacked. It could very well be the professions and life choices we've made because of the abduction. They've put us all in danger at one time or another. You could be borrowing trouble that's not ours."

Declan nodded; again it was a slow one. One filled to the brim with questions that Desmond knew his big brother would still try to answer. But, for now, he seemed to brush off the concern. He tried on a smile. It didn't reach his eyes but it was something.

"I think I might just need a break," he admitted. "I'm starting to lose myself in the job. Even I can see that. I'm starting to copy Dad's habits, the not-good kind. It might be time for a vacation. If only to recharge."

"I think that would be a great idea."

Movement pulled their attention over to the fence next to the stable. Someone was standing on it and smiling back at him. Just like his father once had.

This time it was a different kind of love Desmond felt. One that burrowed into his bones, into his heart and into his soul. His future wife. The mother of their future children. The woman he was ready to spend the rest of his life with.

A mass of dark red curls flew around Riley's head as she waved.

Desmond waved back, unable to not smile.

"I guess their meeting went okay," he said. "Which means I'm on the hook to take her out to Red Oak for a celebratory drink or two tonight."

Not that he minded at all.

Desmond turned back to his brother. Declan was smiling.

"You know another way to help keep the stress off?" Desmond couldn't help but ask. "Finally find someone who keeps that scowl off your face. At the very least I think it's safe to say that, if you have to borrow trouble, having someone by your side sure does help keep you sane."

Declan snorted.

"I might take a short break from work but I don't think I have time for all of that."

Desmond threw his head back in laughter, really feeling it in his heart. He reached over between their horses and managed to clap his brother on the shoulder.

When Desmond spoke again, he might have been staring at Declan, but all he could see was his very own siren.

"When you find the right one, you'll make the time."

He tipped his cowboy hat to his brother and felt

the thrill of riding take over as he and Winona started to gallop.

He could already hear Riley laughing before he ever got to the fence.

* * * * *

*Look for the next book in Tyler Anne Snell's
Winding Road Redemption miniseries,*
Last Stand Sheriff,
on sale next month.

*And don't miss the previous books
in the miniseries:*

Reining in Trouble
Credible Alibi

Available now from Harlequin Intrigue!

Get 4 FREE REWARDS!

We'll send you 2 FREE Books plus 2 FREE Mystery Gifts.

Harlequin Presents books feature the glamorous lives of royals and billionaires in a world of exotic locations, where passion knows no bounds.

FREE
Value Over
$20

Get 4 FREE REWARDS!

We'll send you 2 FREE Books plus 2 FREE Mystery Gifts.

Worldwide Library books feature gripping mysteries from "whodunits" to police procedurals and courtroom dramas.

FREE Value Over $20
